Winter: The Homecoming Blitz

Catarina M. Szymanski

to anyone who has doubted themselves, in love or
otherwise. *(myself included)*

1.

The drive through town is always my favorite at Christmas. Fairy lights wrapping the tall, black lamp posts that lit up the streets at nightfall, wreaths hanging on every door and store windows filled with reds, greens and all-around pure magic on main street. I don't even mind the crisp cold as long as the sun is shining and bright. I slow down in the car to take this moment in. It's been over four years since I left my charming hometown and I have missed it dearly. The flower shop where one can find the most beautiful bouquets all year round, I see the baskets adorning the sidewalk, the explosion of color making that side of the street even more stunning. A few seconds later, I'm passing by the bakery, my mouth instantly watering, remembering how crunchy their bread is. I've never found a good match for it. People are outside despite the cold, having friendly conversations with their neighbors, enjoying a hot drink, all snug in their scarves, and main street never felt so welcoming.

When I see the red-painted building nearer and nearer, my heart races with excitement. I pull up in front of the only Irish pub in town, my dad's pub, proudly named Gallagher's and I can't wait to surprise him. I'm finally back in town, after being gone for long, too long.

The chime from the doorbell takes me back to my childhood and teenage years spent running in and out of this place, meeting friends for hot chocolate and helping dad with orders when I turned 16. The oak-beer smell assaults my nose at first, like it always does, but it's followed by boiled potatoes, gravy, and roast. My stomach does a little backflip, ready for the authentic pub food I've been missing for the last few years. I know to go directly towards the kitchen, where I'll for sure find mom trying to control dad's recipes, just as she's been doing for over 25 years.

"Don't you even think of adding that to my stew!" Dad shoves her aside and I can't help but feel like I'm right at home.

"Would you two stop bickering and come hug your favorite daughter?"

Dad turns around as if he's 20 again, and comes rushing, wrapping me in a hug.

"Tee, why didn't you tell us you were coming into town today?" I hear my mom ask behind my dad, "Move over, it's my time to hug her now, you weren't the one pushing for 20 hours, I should get priority rights."

My dad finally lets me go and I hug my mom just as tightly. I've missed them. "Still adding a zero to that, aren't we, mom?" I tease her. "I didn't want to ruin the surprise. And I'm here just in time for lunchtime, it seems..." My eyes devour everything I see around the kitchen, my stomach definitely complaining now that I haven't fed it in a few hours. "Can I get some stew? Did you make black pudding too? I haven't had one in forever! No one knows how to make it just right."

"Go sit down, and we'll bring it over, dear." Dad's eyes shine through his words, "I'm so happy you're here now, mo stór, especially for Christmas."

Christmas is a really big deal here and we've always spent it as a family. I couldn't not show up this year, I've already missed too many, even if it took me a while to get here and I don't love driving in winter. There's a part of me who's very excited to be back, though.

To see the familiar faces I grew up with. I've already made plans to meet with my best friends, and I can't wait to go into all the Christmas shops that are always extra magical the week before Christmas day.

Moving towards the counter, I sit in one of the high stools, its familiar creaking noise welcoming me home. I close my eyes for a few moments and inhale the smells around me, the food I can almost taste, the oak wood from every surface, the beer spilled somewhere and the coffee brewing. The smells I grew up with, fresh and warm at the same time.

Welcome home, Gallagher's says. I'm happy to be here, I answer back.

When I step outside, the cold air greets me happily, and I decide to take a stroll before going back to the house to unpack. I still have to get almost everyone Christmas gifts as I didn't have the time back in Connecticut, but it's a week before Christmas Eve and one trip downtown will sort me out.

The town vibrates with color and magic; I can feel everyone's enthusiasm without having to talk to them. The holidays truly bring everyone together.

After going into a few stores, including a cute little boutique that wasn't there when I was still in high school, I am content and exhausted. I didn't buy any gifts this time, but I'll be back for a couple that I know will make someone happy. Driving home, I take a different route and pass by all the places I grew up in, the bookstore where my friends and I would spend hours searching for the best romance novels, the photobooth stall that saw more of our faces than our parents did in 7th grade, the Swing by the lake where he told me he loved me for the first time, and the corner shop where we used to go to after school for lemonade and candy on a hot day. I almost drive by his parents' house, but I turn right instead and a couple of minutes later, I'm in my parents' driveway. I take a few slowing breaths, realizing my heart rate jumped up out of nowhere, gather some bags, my purse and my suitcase and enter my childhood home. Nothing's changed, and yet everything has.

Feeling much brighter and clean after a long shower, I start to unpack my suitcase, placing clothes into empty drawers and hanging some nicer dresses and my coat. I'm staying for a couple of weeks, until right after New Year's Eve, so I had to bring a few things over since I had taken almost everything with me when I left to go to university. Maybe I should leave a few items here this time, some things I won't probably need for the next few months. I still haven't made my mind up yet about whether to try to find a job in Connecticut when I finish my internship in the summer, or if I'll move back home for a few months and decide then what to do. Either way, I still have more than half a year, so it's not like I have to make a decision right now. I'm sure mom and dad would love to have me back for a period longer than a few days at a time - since moving north, I never came back but my parents have visited me a few times over the years. I didn't want to let them spend even more money after having paid for my moving trip, and I preferred to have them come to me, anyway. So, they're pretty excited I'm back for a whole two weeks this time around. I'm not too sure how I feel about it yet, but I'm hoping my unease will soon disappear.

Making my way to the bathroom again to apply some makeup, I look in the mirror and am pretty happy with my simple burgundy sweater and gray jeans; all it's missing is maybe a pop of black, so I might have to find a belt, but I'm only meeting Sienna and Liv, and we're mostly homebodies, so we like to be comfortable even when going out to the pub. Well, not that the pub is considered a fancy affair, but everyone has their thing, and I've seen it all in the years working there: from formal attire to people coming in their pajamas thinking no one will notice. And some wouldn't, especially if it's after 10pm on a Friday night.

I grab my heeled black ankle boots, a long scarf and shoot my best friends a quick text saying I'm leaving and will be there in about 10 minutes.

The drive back into town goes smoother now, probably because I'm sticking to the main roads this time, but I can't let my body react every time I pass by an old memory. There are too many of those to let it betray me like that, I wouldn't have a body left in the two weeks I'll be staying here, so, *no more* reacting, body.

The sweet chime welcomes me for the second time today and I immediately see my best friends in the back booth, where we always used to sit making plans for the future and promises of always remaining friends. The promises were kept, the plans not so much.

"I can't believe my ears, Liv! The mouth you've got on you!" Sienna's face has turned all red, and I'm afraid she'll want to hide under the table if Liv continues to share her more adventurous experiences.

"S, how does she still shock you by this point? You should know what to expect from Liv's stories after a decade of knowing her."

"I always think I know what she'll say, but she's got a way of surprising me with every word that comes out of her mouth!" she complains.

"Okay, okay, calm down, S, I won't tell you about my nightly escapades anymore. So," she taps the tabletop, "enough about me, what about our smart girl? Have you *finally* hooked up with someone at Yale?"

"I feel like I've also told you this a thousand times, Liv, I have been on dates and I have fun and that's it. I'm perfectly happy the way I am, and I don't have time for anything else at the moment."

She rolls her eyes at me, showing clearly what she thinks about what I just said. "If you're so happy, then you wouldn't spend your nights rewatching Gilmore Girls for the hundredth time like we know you do. Plus, haven't you found your Logan yet? You should be looking for him outside the classroom, remember? She didn't meet him in the library!"

"For someone who complains I've watched it a lot, you sure seem to know plenty of details about it yourself", I say, hoping she'll feel embarrassed as she always does when admitting she loves Gilmore Girls just as much as Sienna and me.

"Whatever. What I'm trying to say is, don't live your life under the covers, all alone. You gotta jump from the scaffolding sometimes, Tee."

"I appreciate your love and support, but I promise you I'm more than okay and I *am* living my life. I've just been too busy lately to go out and party 'til the morning."

"Speaking of which," Sienna livens up, "let's plan a girls' night out while you're both in town. We could go to the Clubhouse after Christmas, what do you think?"

"Hmmm…", this piques her interest, and Liv continues, "what's gotten you so excited about going to the Clubhouse? If I remember right, you've always said it was the place to go to if you wanted to be felt up or kidnapped. What's changed your mind?"

My ears also perk up. Sienna has never really enjoyed clubbing, even if she always agreed to go out with us dancing. This opinion seems…new.

"Well, it's not like I *hated* the place, but I've heard they changed owners, so it's a more controlled place now. They check cards at the entrance and everything", she says brushing it off.

"It sounds like fun," Liv says in the most monotone voice I've ever heard her use to talk about going out dancing.

We continue catching up for a while, drinking a couple of pints and devouring a platter of finger food, until we all decide we should order some actual food. I go for a pub's staple, a beef burger in a peppercorn sauce with a side of fries. The perfect meal to have while drinking beer, if you ask me. It doesn't hurt it's one of my dad's favorite sauces to make, so I know it'll be delicious.

When the food arrives, which I don't help out with - dad's orders to "just sit down with my friends and enjoy the night" -, we each dig in and the conversation dies out for a few minutes.

After a while, Sienna asks without meeting my eyes, "Tee, have you… Have you thought about *whom* you might run into while you're in town?"

I knew this would be coming up. No point in arguing, they're my best friends, they know me well and it's not like he's the one *who cannot be named.*

I sigh, "I know. It's definitely possible if he also comes back for the holidays, but I can't think about that. No good comes from worrying from anticipation. Whatever happens, happens, and I'll be rea…" My words get cut short when I feel a wave of silence hit us, sucking the air out of the room. I realize the doorbell chimed, I look behind me and I see the reason for the heaviness in the room. My ears start ringing, my heart is throbbing against my throat, and I feel flustered and chilly at the same time.

"…dy." It slips out of my lips. But I know the words don't have a drop of truth when my eyes lock with his.

Knox is back.

I'm *not* ready.

2.

The pub feels smaller all of a sudden, the large distance separating us seeming only a few mere inches. I can almost touch his face.

I shake these thoughts off, my eyes slipping away first, and the sounds return to their normal volume. The voices spread all around our table, ricocheting against the dark wood on the walls, the clinking of beer glasses, something sizzling behind the kitchen doors, and as if the sounds attacking me right now weren't loud enough, my heart beats louder than them all.

I pinch the soft skin between my thumb and index, a technique I've learned in my meditation class, to bring me back to the present, to regain my senses. My body relaxes, letting go, and I feel my feet touch the floor beneath me, the noise lowers to a normal volume and I can look at my friends' faces again.

"Are you okay, Tee?" Liv is the first one to ask. Sienna's face is creased in concern, and her hand touches mine, making me even more present.

I try to smile. "Yeah, I'm okay. I just didn't think all I had to do was say I was ready to see him again and the universe would throw that theory at my face the next second."

"Should we say something to him though?" Sienna is always the peacemaker among us three.

"Maybe? I mean, I really don't know how to proceed here…" I struggle with a jumble of thoughts in my head, not really knowing what I should do, say or feel. Maybe it would only be awkward for me and he's forgotten all about it. Or maybe he doesn't even remember who I am. A pang hits me with that last thought. No, of course he remembers me. How could he not?

I shake those thoughts away for what seems the tenth time and look at both of my friends, who are waiting for my next move.

"I guess it would be okay if we said hi to him? I mean, I haven't seen him in a while, but you guys have and a few months ago you told me you're still following each other on social media, so he'll probably be happy to see you."

"Well, not to disappoint your sudden optimism, but he's just left."

I turn around quickly, "Wha-?"

"He got a takeout bag and left. I guess he's back at his parents." Liv says, proving she had been looking at him those few minutes. "People around town always see him at Christmas, Tee, he always comes back for the holidays, he just never actually leaves their house much from what we gathered."

I try to make sense of that information in my mind. My reaction wasn't all that surprising, I haven't seen him in forever. So, I may want to be ready, but that doesn't mean I am. But then again, I still wanted to go up to him and ask him all about his famous career in Chicago. His dream had turned reality, and I read about him a lot in the Sports section. I wouldn't say I was stalking him really, it was more of a healthy interest in how he was doing…and who… He was always spotted with a beautiful, blonde girl, and not just the one, they were always different, and always blonde. I touch my light-brown hair, feeling self-conscious all of a sudden.

He had moved on for sure. I knew that. Liv and Sienna knew that. Our whole town knew that. That was part of the reason I preferred not coming back, half of the town knew about the big shot star who got injured after that one touchdown and everyone still talks about how he still made it work. Half of our town knows the story of the star quarterback who didn't ask the girl to go with him. I noticed the stares and whispers back then, so I'm not quite jumping at the chance of coming back every chance I get. Being here is heavy, there are too many memories, too many feelings.

He didn't come up to us either, I realize. In the midst of my troubled emotions, I almost didn't process that nugget of information. He saw me. I know he saw me, he saw us sitting here. But he chose not to come over. My stomach ties in a knot and the emotions I felt in the weeks leading up to him leaving rush back up. It was his decision. It's been over 4 years since we broke up; I just have to accept it once and for all.

Later that night, back in my childhood bedroom, I relive those seconds that felt like hours. The chime, the whoosh of the door closing, how I felt his presence before looking at him, the way our eyes locked, the fireworks of emotions shooting in my chest and the realization he left without saying anything.

Chime.

Whoosh.

Eyes.

Green, troubled eyes meeting mine.

Fireworks.

And then, nothing.

A brick wall hitting me, dragging me down to Earth. The fireworks show cancelled, the air in the room lifted.

I relive these flashbacks again and again, my eyes closed and the mental pictures going through my brain like a reel, going a mile per minute.

My brain decides to pause them where his eyes met mine, I can feel a wave from the top of my head to the bottom of my feet, the intensity of his gaze, stripping me down. But just like a wave, crashing, the moment was soon swallowed back into the ocean, no marks left on the sand, forgotten. I rewind to my body turning towards the door, his eyes land on mine, a wave crashes into my body, and is washed away.

I fall asleep with thoughts of green eyes, the beach and wishful permanent writings in the sand.

The next morning, I wake up tired. I had dreams all night which, whenever happens, leaves me feeling like I haven't slept at all. Coffee is the first thing on my agenda then. Before kicking the sheets, my mind slips away to last night. *No!* I won't let you live through it again, brain. You've done enough.

Annoyed with myself, I kick the sheets harder than I have to and jump to my feet. Coffee it is.

Downstairs, I find an empty kitchen. The clock shows it's after 10, so both mom and dad will already be at the pub serving breakfast. I don't feel like going back there yet, so I spend the rest of the morning walking around the house, staring at walls I've seen all my life but, yet look different. I check my emails and surely find a couple from one professor who seems to work day and night, no matter if it's the holidays. I'll answer him when I'm back, I promised myself I wouldn't do any work while here.

In my room, I find a box with old things. I find some old diaries from when Liv and I were 8 and decided to share our emotions in the same notebook. We thought this way we could keep up with everything that was happening in each other's lives, even if we lived in the same street and went to the same schools. We were 8, what can you do. I take a few photos of some passages and share them in our group chat. Sienna aptly named it 'the three musketeers' even though none of us has ever read the book, nor watched the movie.

After a few laughs reading about our problems in primary school, I go through more items in the box and at the bottom, I find his old red and black jersey. I'm a walking cliché, so I bring it to my nose and inhale it. I didn't actually expect it to smell like him, but it somehow does and tears pool at my eyes.

I put it back in the box and notice something else tucked inside a jewelry box, a letter I hadn't seen in over 4 years. It doesn't matter now. I fold it again and hide it away.

Enough of reminiscing for today. I take a quick shower, carefully washing off my face so I don't forget to do it and grab a pair of comfy leggings I had left here and a jumper. I let my hair fall down my back, brush the knotty waves, and decide to wear it down today. I want to take the day off to do some light reading and maybe pop by the pub later in the evening. I've decided I don't feel like going back yet, and I don't have to feel like a coward, I'm just taking some time off for myself and my feelings, that's perfectly healthy and balanced.

I'm sure my meditation teacher would congratulate me on this step. It's a 'me day', and I deserve a few of those.

3.

It's the coldest day of the season yet, a day in late February, and I can't believe they won't cancel the game tonight. Ox says football waits for no one nor good weather, but I still thought the coaches of both teams wouldn't let them play. But I guess I should know better. Both towns are too invested in this game and there are talks of college scouts attending it, so no one wants to miss that opportunity. We've only been dating a few months, but I know that, especially Knox, would not miss this opportunity, it means too much for him.

"I think you're going to freeze your ass off tonight, Oxie, and then what will I slap when I see you?", I giggle on the phone.

"If that happens, I'll give you something else to slap, babe."

He can be such a smart mouth when he wants to, but I can't hide my smile when I say, "You better not freeze your best asset off. I can't believe you guys are still playing, though. Won't the ground be too sleek in the evening?"

"Ina, I know you worry about us, but it'll be okay. Remember that time we played against the Wolfs and there was a storm, and thunders flashing through the sky? We still made it, no one got hurt, we're trained for this. Anyway, we need to play, it might be our last chance to show off to some college scouts."

"I remember...", it trails off my lips. That had been a scary night in his junior year. Ox and I still weren't dating nor had officially met, but that night my eyes didn't leave him. I couldn't stop my body from feeling every tackle, every hit, every fall. He had done amazing that night. Played with raw talent and a lot of work too. I think that was one of the first times I realized I couldn't stop staring at him, on and off the field.

"I remember that night, Ox. Of course, I remember. Just be safe tonight, okay? I'll be on the stands cheering for you."

"I'll come meet you after the game. Love you 3000, Ina." That always made my heart lighter.

"Love you 3000, Oxie."

Knox had a long list of superstitions he had to go through before each game, and one of the biggest ones was not talking to anyone in the half an hour preceding the beginning of the game. I always made fun of him and teased him about it, but I got it. I had my own things. I couldn't go into an exam without my blue ring that I got with Liv and Sienna when we officially became best friends in middle school. We each had gotten a simple band, painted in our favorite color. Mine was blue, Liv's was purple and Sienna's yellow. We promised we would always wear them, but especially in stressful and tough times, so we would always remember we had each other's backs. So, I wore mine at every test. I also had to watch an episode of Gilmore Girls the night before a big event - there was something about it that always calmed me down. And I had a lucky black belt that I was wearing the day Knox and I talked for the first time. I wore it every time he had a game, just like this evening.

I finished looping the belt into my jeans and fluffed my hair for the twelfth time. I always got extra nervous when Knox had a game. I wanted him to succeed so badly that it was as if I was the one who had to throw the ball and make the right gameplay. He had so much relying on this game too. He's two years older than me, so this is his last chance at getting drafted to play college football. I also felt some pressure from the cliques at school. I hated how cliché my life sounded at times, but yes, I was the smart, straight-As type of girl who fell in love with the quarterback. But the cliché stopped there. I wasn't a poor little girl who was too naive to defend herself if needed, I was Irish, after all. I'm the one who approached Knox one day after school and asked him if he wanted to hang out at the Swing - which was what we called the small park by the lake, famous for its wide swing that can seat two or three people - and he was the one who was a little taken aback and didn't know what to say right away. Long story short, I still felt the pressure to be the 'cliché quarterback's girlfriend', dress in mini-skirts and become a cheerleader. Welcome to high school, Tee, where time seems stuck in a rom-com from the 90s, even in the 21st century.

I couldn't care less tonight, though. I had my lucky belt and Knox had his own ritual going on, so nothing would be amiss. The college scouts would love him and he would get multiple college scholarships to play football. He would finally be able to relax and just focus on his dream.

I wandered off into the kitchen and made some peanut butter, nutella sandwiches because they're Knox's favorite and he was always ready for a banquet after a game. I packed a couple of orange juice boxes too, and I sent a text to my mom and dad telling them I was off to the game and would most likely meet them at the pub after.

The drive to school was quick and soon I was sitting next to Liv and Sienna, us three dressed in red and black, our school's colors. I had put on my black jeans, black Uggs and lucky black belt and then put on the warmest red sweater I found in my closet and my thick black winter coat. I had a red beanie on and gloves, but I could still feel how cold it was.

The atmosphere was exhilarating, everyone from our school cheering as loud as they could against the other team's fans, but my mind was still on how icy the ground should be and how safe it would be for the players. They really do anything for football.

'I can't believe we have to stand here for the next couple of hours, Tee! I hope you'll make it up to us with some free food at the pub after!" Sienna was pouting. She wasn't the biggest football enthusiast, and I knew she only came to the games for me. Before Knox and I started dating, us three would never be seen here, we would probably be lounging at each other's homes, eating candy and popcorn while TVD was on. Sienna had a thing for Damon - I mean, who wouldn't, but she was on another level.

'I'm sorry, girls, I really wish we wouldn't have to be here tonight either. It's too cold, but they have to play, it's an important game for both teams." I try to negotiate.

Our team's losing by 5. There are 33 seconds left in the timer, and Knox decides to surprise everyone by taking the play himself. Everyone shoots up from their seats, holding their breath watching a quarterback run for the 20-yard line, then 10 yards.

Knox flies over a player and lands a few inches beyond the goal line just when the timer goes off. Everyone is jumping up and down and cheering the millisecond he touches the ground, which makes it hard for some to see what happens then. A player from the other team who had also jumped to tackle Ox lands directly on his knee and you could almost hear the crack through the arena.

Everyone goes radio silent for a few seconds, Knox gets up, smiles and throws his arm in the air - our school goes wild, cheering, and soon his teammates are hugging him and celebrating their victory.

I run down the few stairs and into the field and go straight for him.

He sees me and opens his arms as if to say, 'you see, we got it, I told you so." I hug him first and then yell above the shouts and celebrations, "Seems like we got ourselves a superstar among us. Shall I bow down to you, Oxie?"

His smile stretches across his face, and he lifts me up in the air before saying, "I shall be the one to bow down to you forever, babe, and don't call me Oxie in public. People will think I'm a softie, babe." He teases, and then proceeds to spin us around, as if Oxie wasn't appropriate for a big boy like him but spinning in joy like a child was.

His face contorts with the first spin, and he loses his balance for a second before putting me down. "Ouch. I guess that's gonna bruise. Did you see that Tanner guy from the other team who tackled my knee when I was already down? What an asshole!" he shakes his head, "I gotta ice this before it swells."

I look at his face, listening to his words and worry is all over my mine when I say, "Does it hurt? Should you ask the doctor to check it out?"

"Nah, babe, I'll get inside and ask the coach for an ice pack. Here. Keep this," he removes his very sweaty shirt and gives it to me, "Now you have something else to get lucky." He winks at me and starts walking towards the locker room.

"You better not think I'll get lucky in this stinky old jersey!" I shout back at him.

I cannot not notice the way he tries to not put weight on his right leg. I hope he won't need to sit out in the next game, they're so close to the finals, it would devastate him.

The following months were brutal. Knox got offers to different colleges, but he needed surgery after that last tackle - an ice pack didn't cure it after all -

so he wouldn't be able to play for a few, long months. His doctor told him he would need physical therapy and a lot of patience, but that chances were, he would recover at 100% if he rested and followed doctor's orders. He didn't get to play for the rest of the season, and by the end of the school year, we found out therapy would not be enough after all, and his surgery was booked for the summer. I couldn't help but rejoicing a little bit in the fact that I would get him for a little while longer. After recovering from the surgery and a few months of physical therapy again, he would probably go to a big, fancy college far away and I wouldn't see him again.

But those were thoughts I couldn't allow myself to have. For now, I had him with me, my lucky belt and my new (washed 5 times and half a bottle of his perfume later) lucky red and black jersey.

4.

I can't hide the fact that I pulled out the shirt I found in the box again and smelled it for another 10 minutes before dumping it in the back of my closet and closing the door. That's when I realized I had spent too many hours locked in the house and maybe now was a great time to go back out and enjoy the fresh air.

The thoughts of the past haunted me every single step. The memories were still so fresh, not like they had happened years ago, but only a few *minutes* ago. I could see him, I could still feel his touch, his smell and his taste. I forced myself time and time again to return to reality, to the present, but those memories made me want to go back, to stay in the past with him.

After half an hour of agonizing flashbacks, I decide it's time to go by the pub and get something to eat. The town has too many marks of him, and us, every corner I pass, I feel like there's a memory yelling in my face. It's too exhausting, so the pub seems like the right choice, even though I'm still recovering from my last time there.

My parents have always loved Knox, but they weren't too keen on us dating when they believed I was supposed to be working towards a ticket out of town and 'get an education', like dad always said. They warmed up to the idea eventually, but in the first months before his injury, we were always running around town or at the Swing just spending some time together. But we rarely went to the pub just us two, since we had other ideas in mind of a better way to spend an afternoon off school. So the pub seemed like the right choice right now.

The warm air welcomes me, and the familiarity of the place always makes me forget about everything else, so Knox is out of my mind after I step inside.

"Hi, ma, what you doing out here? Shouldn't you be at the back telling dad he's doing something wrong?" I tease her.

"I've nagged him enough for today, honey, and we are one short out here tonight. Mia didn't show up for her shift again, so I'm helping out. What are you doing here? Got hungry?"

"You could've called me, mom, I would have come in earlier to help."

"I know you would, and that's why I didn't call. Now, dad made some stew, do you want me to get you some?" my parents are the best, that's why I didn't want to leave them and move so far away. But they said more than half of our town was counting on me to become a famous architect, so I could come back one day and design new buildings around town.

"I'd love some, and I'll go get it myself. Say hi to dad while I'm at it." I told her while already halfway towards the kitchen.

To be fair, I was happy she hadn't called because the mere thought of running into him again and have him not say a word to me would probably send me down a spiral. And being back here didn't help after all. The encounter was too fresh in my mind, and I realized I was a little scared he might show up again.

So, kitchen it is for me. I push the door open and immediately see my dad around a huge pot that looks like it could feed the entire town plus the one over. "Something smells delicious in here, dad, and I'm not talking about the fresh flowers I see mom put everywhere."

"That woman will kill me one day! She does this on purpose, you know? She brings the flowers in here because she knows I'll start sneezing and have to step away for some time, and then she can sneak in and add more spices to my stew!", he says while continuing to stir the pot, "Do you want a bowl? It's ready, I was just making sure it isn't too spicy."

"Dad, I'm sure she doesn't think your stew needs more spices, she loves your stew," I lie, "She just told me to have some while I'm here. And yes, please, give me a bowl."

It's everything I know it to be. So many flavors and depth to it, "You really make the best stew, dad, I can't get anything remotely similar in New Haven," this one is the full truth.

He smiles, proud of himself, and the next few moments are spent with me devouring the stew (and getting a second, heaping bowl) and him tidying his workspace.

"I overheard the girls talk about last night, Tee. Him walking in here while you were having dinner. Are you okay, tootsie?" his eyes bleed worry, yet his voice is soft like when you see a bird and move slowly to not scare him off.

"Dad, first of all, don't call me tootsie, I'm 22. And... I'm okay", I convince myself more than him, "It's okay. It's not like I expected him to change his mind now and just run to me in slow motion like in a rom-com."

"That doesn't mean you can't be upset. You have every right to feel something, even if it's been years since he left. Feelings don't just disappear, they play hide-and-seek sometimes, but they show up unannounced when you bump into that tree that was your favorite hiding spot. Know what I mean, tootsie?"

"Yeah, dad, I know what you mean... I can't say I expected anything different from the situation, but I'll admit there was a tiny part of me that wished he would apologize, boombox above his head and all. But that part of me lives in fairyland with Tom Hanks. Or Gerard Butler, actually, and that fairyland becomes PS: I *still* love you."

I sigh, memories of him taking me to the drive-in theater most Saturday nights where they broadcast the cheesiest rom-coms, all the way from the 90s to How to Lose a Guy in 10 Days. I still don't know how anyone could lose Matthew McConaughey on purpose, but

Knox got a motorbike after watching that one with me and noticing how hot I got with that last taxi-motorbike chasing scene. He said he would motorbike chase me for the rest of our lives.

Well, that didn't quite come true, now, did it?

I notice apprehension written all over dad's face, "It's okay, dad, it's been far too long, and I'll be okay. It just took me by surprise, really."

The rest of the night until closing time, my heart stopped every time that damn bell would chime, and I was this *close* to stepping on a stool and yanking it off the wall with my bare hands. I hated my body for betraying my brain that way, but I decided to attribute the stupid reaction to PTSD from last night. It's not like the idiot would know it wasn't supposed to react to simple triggers, and my brain was getting a little mushy too, not filtering memories like the kisses, his hands, his spontaneous actions, his romantic words and the way he always smiled when he saw me in the morning. He would blush slightly, a tiny dimple formed in his right cheek and his perfect teeth would greet me. I thought it would be a thing just for the honeymoon phase, but he did it even a whole year after we started dating. He would light up my whole day too, making my heart flutter even after the 6 months I spent nursing him in his bedroom after his surgery every single day from the moment he woke up until he passed out again. I saw a lot of his bodily functions during that time, so I surprised even myself when I felt like I could do it all over again and felt a tad sad when he could move well again because that meant our days watching movies, studying and talking about the future would be over.

Hell, I still smiled even today thinking about him and our memories. Even after he left me without a glance back. Even after he crushed my heart into a powdery mess, even after the constant gossip magazines covers with his face swallowing a girl's mouth. I still felt the little backflip of my stomach hearing his name, still smiled hearing him talk after games on TV, still held my breath every time he got tackled and stood back up. The sad thing was I didn't expect to see him yesterday, not in the flesh, mere feet away from me, but I had never stopped seeing him in my thoughts, my dreams… and my TV.

5.

After yet again a troubled sleep with dreams of mysterious green eyes and playful smiles, I get up and take a cold shower. Stepping out after freezing my ass off, I take a look in the mirror and notice the dark bags under my eyes and my dull skin. Great, as if I didn't have enough going on being back, I now have to start worrying about anti-aging creams and a high coverage concealer. Maybe that could be my morning plan. Go out into town, hit a couple drugstores and maybe book a fresh cut at the salon. That should cheer me right up.

I open the 'three musketeers' group chat and ask them both if they'd like to have a pampering morning. Liv is quick to answer and says she's up for it. Sienna only answers once I'm done getting dressed and brushing my hair, which I realize now I could have just washed at the salon.

Three seconds later, Liv's calling me. "What's that all about?" she yells in my ear.

"I just read it, like you, so how should I know?" I answer after putting her on speaker.

"Where is she? I don't recall any friends she might have in Providence, so what is she doing there this early?"

"I don't know, Liv, maybe she went gift shopping?" I suggest.

"Gift shopping in Providence? What is she buying there that she can't buy here?"

"Liv, I'm telling you I have no idea, why are you asking me these questions as if I'm Sienna's bodyguard?" Liv has never done well not being kept in the loop of our lives. She believes she has the right to know every single thing about us because, as she puts it, she tells us every detail of her life. She's not wrong, she does share everything. Too much, if you ask Sienna.

"Anyway, shall we meet in 15 at the salon?" I ask before she interrogates me further.

"Sure, I'm ready, I'll leave in 5."

After we hang up, I go downstairs to get my bag and a chocolate muffin to eat on the way there. The sky's clear, but the temperature is rather low for December. I should've worn a scarf to keep me warmer if we end up walking around town after the salon.

The drive into town is uneventful, and I spot Liv's car in front of the salon, so I park next to her.

"Hi!" she says cheerfully.

"Are you feeling better about not knowing everything about Sienna's life?" I tease her.

She is staring at me like I hurt her feelings, "Absolutely not! I will investigate further until I find out the truth. She's been acting weird," she says in a low voice, "The other night we got together before you arrived, she listened to my most recent hookup *without* saying a word", her face showing just how shocked she feels.

"Maybe she was so happy to see you, she didn't want to be rude."

"Tee, she heard the words 'butt plug' and she didn't even stop me then!" she shouts at me.

Liv does have a point, though. That doesn't sound like something Sienna would just happily hear and continue the conversation as if Liv had said the words "Sunday brunch" - something was up. "I guess we'll have to give her some time to share whatever's going on then, if something is indeed going on. Don't be an a-hole about it and let her be", I scold her.

She puffs, not happy with my answer, but lets it go. "Let's go in, I'm gonna turn into a popsicle soon."

The salon is never crowded on a Monday morning, so I was surprised when an hour later, all chairs were taken, and the gossip was flowing freely like rosé on a girls' bottomless brunch. "Triona, I'm so happy to see that you're back in town, honey. How's everything up in Connecticut? Are you making us all proud there?" Mrs. Reid asks me, her kind voice reminding me of the little cakes she always kept at her home for the little kids who stopped by after school.

"Everything is going well, Mrs. Reid, thank you for asking. I'm almost done with school, and I already have an internship lined up this upcoming summer at one of the hippest agencies in the city! And I'll be able to keep my dorm those extra months, so it was a great opportunity", I'm beaming, it really is an amazing opportunity and I can't wait to start actually working and designing homes.

"Good job, dear!", Mrs. Reid says warmly, "Be sure to not forget us old people here and come build a retirement home with a pool, so I can live the rest of my life happy and tan."

Mrs. Reid was always the kindest old lady. "For you, I'll build you your own home with a pool, Mrs. Reid, as long as you keep baking those little cakes I used to eat after school," I tease her.

"You've got yourself a deal!" Mrs. Reid says from the hot rollers chair, looking very serious.

I spend the next quarter of an hour scrolling through my phone, liking videos of puppies clicking on a mat that allowed them to speak to their parents and couples dancing to Latin music. Honestly, you couldn't go wrong with puppies and a little Latin music. Maybe the couples' part of it was also interesting, but I wouldn't admit that to anyone, not even myself.

"Hey, Liv, when do you think was the last time we went out dancing?"

She thinks for a few seconds before answering, "Way too long for an immediate answer. Why do you ask? Are you feeling like rubbing your ass against some tattooed-up asshole who smells too well for his own damn good and who will most likely never see your face again after you flee his apartment the next morning in such a rush you leave behind your favorite hook-up panties?"

The whole salon quiets down, staring at her. My entire face blushes thinking of Mrs. Reid listening to this. To my demise, Liv continues, "Damn, it's been too long since I've been properly rub-"

"Hey! Liv! Hey! *Ha-ha*, you're funny. She's just joking around, this Liv," I apologize to the dozen eyes staring in our direction.

"Well, you girls are young, you should definitely be waking up in various beds from time to time. However, I'm not too sure what to think about this gentleman with tattoos and him not wanting to see your lovely faces again," Mrs. Reid surprises us by saying.

That just fuels Liv some more. "Damn right, Mrs. Reid, he should be ringing up my phone non-stop! Not that I would answer, but the gesture's in the small details, ain't it?" She smiles proudly. Of what, I'm not entirely sure, but knowing Liv, she's most likely feeling proud of not being one to cry over a guy who she'll never see again after a great night out. Sometimes, I wish I was a little more like her. More carefree, maybe. Not dwell on what a certain someone is up to, or stalk him online while rubbing, not against *someone*, but my hand. God, I do need to get out more. What would Liv say if she knew I've been pining over him all these years and staring at his photos and interviews while reaching climax. What an effing loser. Kn- nope - I refuse to say his name even in my thoughts -, *HE* probably doesn't even remember what I sound like, after all the different women he's made scream in his bed. Go away, thoughts. I hate the visuals that tag along from imagining your ex in bed with other people.

"Are you listening to me?" Liv slaps my thigh.

I wake up from those nightmare thoughts and shake myself. "Yes, I'm listening, go ahead." I smile encouragingly at her - *and* myself.

"I was saying it's been too long since we've all gone out together, but we talked about going to the Clubhouse while we're in town, remember? Before *you know who* showed up at the pub," she whispers that last part.

That feels like another slap, but I try to roll with it. "Sure, I know! I was just thinking that it has been quite a while since I've gone dancing just for fun, shake my worries away, you know?"

"Well, you're in luck, coz we'll be shaking it so much, the whole club might come crumbling down."

I laugh at that. Liv might swear like a sailor and share a little too much, but she's been my best*est* friend for too long, and she always knows how to perk me up.

Once we're both almost ready, Liv's just getting one last portion of hair blown out, I make my way to the till to pay. I hear the door open and a familiar voice sings towards me.

"Triona! Oh my word, you *are* in town! I've heard some people mention it, but I couldn't believe it until I saw it myself. How are you, dear?" she means people have explicitly gone to her, the biggest gossiper in town, to tell her the prodigal daughter has finally returned home.

"Hi, Miss Patty. I'm great, thanks. How are you? How's the flower business, still blooming?"

"Oh, dear, you and your puns. I see nothing's changed," I'm not sure whether to take that as a compliment, but she continues, "The shop's doing well, thank you. You know, there's always a wedding, a funeral, someone gets sick. There's always a need for flowers!" she speaks loudly, as if the entire salon wasn't already listening to her every word, "Now, I hope I'm not intruding, but I also heard Knox is in town. Did you know that, dear? Oh, what a pity everything that happened, really. We all thought you would be married by now, you know. I'd have personally made your bouquet! I can already imagine it, red roses, and white lilies." Don't ask me how she managed to say all that without pausing to breathe. That was Miss Patty for you. She would not give you time for throwing a little word in, with how fast she spoke.

I struggled with what to say, but settled for what I could come up with in that second, aware everyone's ears were waiting for me, "Right, I heard he's in town, yes. And Miss Patty, we really wouldn't have gotten married because he's a big star and I just want to design buildings, you see. Also, I really hate roses, and anything red, sorry to burst your bubble." Did I say too much? I said too much. I wouldn't be surprised if this interaction was in the paper tomorrow morning.

Mortified, I pay for what I owe and move towards the door, "Liv, I'll wait for you outside. Thanks, Clara! And good to see you again, Mrs. Reid. Ladies…" I almost curtsy and then remember we're not in the 40s, so I just leave and let the cold air to hit me.

6.

I can't believe they're still hung up on what happened 4 years ago. I mean, we were kids. No one ends up with their high school sweetheart anymore, this isn't *Twilight*.

I'm still cooling off when I hear Liv's voice behind me, "Hey, you okay?" She looks at me with concern written all over her face.

"Yeah. I'm okay. Let's go, I still wanna do some Christmas shopping."

We spend the next couple of hours hitting every drugstore in town, buying makeup I definitely don't need - I mean, how many nude lipsticks does one truly need -, and I end up finding a great gift for mom. We're at this beautiful store filled with knickknacks and handmade items that proves to be very successful when shopping for your loved ones. We move towards the checkout, and I immediately recognize a face, "Sarah! Hey! It's been forever since I last saw you! How are you?" I make my way around the till to hug her.

"Oh my God, hi Tee! I didn't know you were in town, otherwise I would have texted you to meet up! How are you? You look beautiful, as always." Sarah was in our class in high school and was always this friendly. We weren't super close, but friends nonetheless, and we used to hang out after school all together by the bleachers. Liv hugs her too and says 'hi'.

"I'm great, thank you! You look great too, what have you been up to?"

"Yeah, and let us know if you can hook us up with free products, everything's great in here!" Liv beams next to me.

"Liv, you also haven't changed a bit," Sarah laughs, "I'm also doing well, I'm actually the owner of this shop, so thank you for your feedback, Liv, but I won't be able to give out freebies, I'm afraid. I opened not so long ago, and I'm yet to make a profit this month."

"Of course we're not looking for freebies, Sarah, don't listen to Liv, she's just being rude," that grants a sneer from Liv, "But she's right. We love your shop, I've found some great gifts for my family. And I'll be sure to come back before I leave for Connecticut and get some things for myself as well."

"Thank you, girls. That's very sweet of you." She starts scanning my items when she seems to remember something, "Oh! I don't know if you guys got a text from Matt, you know, Matt Clark from the football team, he probably doesn't know you're in town, but he planned a bonfire night like we used to have in the summer. Would you like to go? I'm gonna go!"

"Sure, when is it?" Liv has all but forgotten about the freebies once given the chance to hook up with someone from high school. I'm pretty sure that's one type of guy she has on her "to-do" list, as in, to actually *do*, and hasn't crossed out yet. 'High school old buddy' is probably right above 'Guy with a piercing on his junk' and below 'Virgin', which she's told me she has crossed out already - but which one I can't remember.

"It's gonna be Wednesday night at the usual place, by the lake. Should start around 6, bring some drinks if you'd like!"

"We'll be there!", Liv screams, not giving me any room for an answer myself.

We leave the shop and I can see she's all too happy with herself, "Don't tell me you're about to cross one of your "to-do" guys, please. We know everyone who's gonna be there, and I honestly cannot recall a single guy you'd wanna do 5 or 6 years ago, so who's it gonna be?" I ask her, making her sweat a little.

"I don't know, Tee, that's the point! We're gonna mingle and be single for the night!"

"We *are* single…"

"Besides the point", she brushes me off, "We're gonna have the best time! I just hope Miss goody two-shoes doesn't bail on us and actually loosens up. That girl is in serious need of her own 'to-do' list."

"Don't talk about Sienna like that, Liv. She'll kick your ass if she finds out you're giving her crap about that. And I'm sure she'll want to come. She loves to reminisce, and she won't mind seeing everyone again."

"That is true, she actually had friends in all the different cliques at school, the horror," she feigns shock but laughs right after. "Hey, now we've got ourselves a dilemma", she goes back to being serious.

"What is that?" something about her face makes me think there truly is a problem I didn't think of.

"What are we going to wear?" she asks, her voice barely above a whisper, her eyes round as saucers.

To her defense, she truly would think this was a dilemma we had to discuss. I'm not gonna lie, I also love planning outfits for different occasions, but Liv has always been on a different league. You wouldn't necessarily guess it by looking at her, but every day she plans what she wears to a T. She's not the walk off a runaway type, but she's not afraid to experiment and loves to go thrifting. Every time, she makes it a competition with herself (when Sienna and I don't tag along) to see if she can find a piece to outdo her last best found.

I try not to roll my eyes blatantly at her. "Yes, Liv, we can spend hours overthinking what we're gonna wear at this bonfire where we don't care about half of the people there and where it'll be dark, so most people won't even notice what we're wearing. Of course we *have* to overanalyze our outfits." This time she catches me and sees the tiniest eye roll in the world.

"Hey! Don't mock me. You know I need to find my next item to tick off there, so I need to look absolutely ravishing. The I-can't-wait-to-lay-you-down-spread-your-legs-and-eat-you-out kind of ravishing," her face is still serious, but her eyes are clouded with what I can only imagine is a memory of said type of ravishing. I instantly wanna gag.

"Could you please not allow your brain to fly over to those memories when we're out in public and you're right next to me? I haven't even had breakfast today, but I feel like yesterday's dinner's looking for a way out."

"Don't be such a prude, Tee, we know how wild you used to be. Focus on used to, though, and the only *one* who took you there", she gives me a 'you-know-who' face.

I do know who. And I do miss those days (and nights) when I felt so carefree, so wild. My heart was in a constant parade, drumming to the beat.

I need to stop letting *my* brain fly away to these thoughts in public. Or at home, for that matter.

"We can't all be living such a thrilling life, Liv, we leave it to the best ones, and you are certainly one of the best ones."

"I won't disagree with that, I am the best one indeed," she smiles from ear to ear, surely with the confidence to beat worthy opponents. "Should we give Sienna a call? Let her know about the bonfire and ask her what she's gonna wear?"

We've been walking around town, towards our cars now that our hands can't carry anything else.

"Let's put our bags in the car and sit inside yours to call her then," I tell her moving towards my old car, opening the trunk to drop my bags inside, then meet her by her car and sit on the passenger's seat.

Sienna answers after a few rings, "Hey, S. I'm with Tee, you're on speaker. We just finished going into twenty thousand stores and bought twenty million gifts," she pauses for dramatic effect, "So, as you can see, our town offers a wide variety of choice for gift shopping," Liv says, clearly wanting to find out more about why Sienna was in Providence earlier this morning.

"Hi, Liv, hi, Tee. I'm doing well, thank you for asking. Congrats on all the shopping, I still haven't finished mine, ugh, it makes me dizzy just thinking about how crowded everywhere must be right now."

Liv stares at me, making hand gestures, which I cannot comprehend. She is frantically pointing at me and the phone and then to herself and making circles around her head. "Wha…?", I wanna ask her before she interrupts me with a death stare.

"So, you're still not done with your Christmas shopping, Sienna?" Liv quits her gesturing and takes charge instead.

"Hmm, no, not really. I might have to step into town tomorrow evening to get a couple of things I forgot," Sienna explains, sounding really annoyed by this.

"And you went to Providence extra early, but you didn't get everything you need? That sounds like b-s to me." Liv's a straight shooter, always.

I can hear the offense Sienna takes by her words. "I don't owe you any explanations!" she sounds upset now. I decide I need to intervene.

"Of course you don't, S. Don't listen to her, she still hasn't had her morning man today," I look over at Liv and her face says she's still unconvinced about Sienna's answer, but doesn't disagree with my words. "Anyway, we're calling you because we were at a store that opened not long ago, apparently, and guess who we met there!"

"Who?"

"Sarah! Do you remember her? From high school?"

"Yeah, of course, I used to work with her after school too."

"Oh, that's right. Well, she didn't know Liv and I were back in town, but once she saw us, she invited us to a bonfire party with our old class."

"Ohh," she doesn't get immediately as excited as we thought she would be, "when will that be?"

I look at Liv, mentally exchanging a few words with her. Sienna does sound odd; she would normally jump at the chance of meeting her old classmates. She really was cool with everyone at school, so between us three, she should be the one happy about this party. And she *loved* bonfire night!

"Hmm, right, it'll be in a couple of days, Wednesday night. Are you thinking of not going? What's up with you?" I try to make a joke of it, not wanting to sound harsh like Liv.

"Oh, nothing. I just have a few things already lined up for the next few days before Christmas, but…" she seems to think about it for a moment, and we can hear some rustling in the background.

"S?"

"Yeah, sorry. I was just looking over my calendar. Yeah, I guess I can say hi to everyone and be there for a couple of hours. That would be okay."

Now it's Liv's turn to squint her eyes at me, and mentally say, 'See, I told you, she's acting weird.'

"O-okay, Sienna! We were just talking about what clothes we're gonna wear. You know how Liv gets with this." I try to change topics.

At that, she laughs. "I bet! Well, considering you've just told me about this, I haven't had time to think about it. Should we meet before and raid Liv's closet together? It'll be like old times!" She sounds excited now, more like the Sienna we know.

Liv also pipes up. "Yeah! Maybe we can find something really slutty for you to wear, and you can finally make out with Andrew after crushing hard on him all those years."

"I did *not* crush on Andrew!" Sienna yells. Liv and I just laugh. Sienna had the worst crush on him for the entire time we attended high school. The type of crush that made her follow him around but never dare to speak to him in full sentences.

"Don't give her shit, Liv", I scold her, as if I hadn't just laughed alongside her.

"Tee, do you think *he's* gonna be there too?" Sienna asks.

That makes me stop laughing, and my breath is knocked out of my lungs because I know she's not asking about Andrew. I hadn't yet thought about that. Of course he would most likely be there. Star player in a little town, back home where half of his hometown *loves* him, and Matt is the one throwing the get-together, they played together for a year and whoever is in town from the football team will probably attend too, so why would he refuse the chance of meeting his old teammates?

"S!" Liv shouts at her through the phone, "Why did you have to mention him?"

"I'm sorry! I just thought you had discussed it already. I mean, it's the second thing that crossed my mind after hearing about bonfire night. He used to throw them himself, remember?"

"It's okay, S, it's not like you single-handedly decided to invite him. Of course he'll be there, right?" I look around looking for a miracle.

"Well, maybe he won't," Sienna says encouragingly, "maybe he'll have to stay home with his parents."

"Or he'll get sick," Liv offers.

"Yeah, or he might not even want to go since now he's such a big shot out there, he probably won't want to hang around us nobodies."

"Yeah…" I exhale slowly. But even in that moment, we all know that he would never think that way about his hometown, nor would he miss a bonfire night. They used to be his favorite.

One day, many, many moons ago, he told me they became his favorite because he had met me there for the first time. I had obviously seen him many times before at school, but he was the quarterback, everyone knew him or *of* him. So, for all purposes, that bonfire night at the end of October of my sophomore year was our meet-cute.

It was also after one of them that, in front of my house, I had told him, for the first time ever, that I loved him, and then proceeded to run hide inside.

He had told me they were his favorite nights. Bonfire nights held a special mystique for us, but I wondered now if he remembered them as vividly as I did.

7.

Sienna and I had arrived at Liv's parents' house over 2 hours ago, but none of us was ready. I looked at the clock on the bedside table and it already marked 6:08. Not that we had to be on time, but I've always been a stickler for good time keeping, and I hated being late for this type of events. I needed my time to scourge the place, see where the best hanging around places were and feel the space. I'm not gonna lie, I liked to know where the best spot was to see whoever arrive, him possibly showing up, a sure reason to make me want to be there before everyone else even more.

"C'mon, Liv, let's just throw some clothes on and let's gooooooooo!", I shake her arm, pleading like a little kid, "I hate being late! You know that."

"We're all aware of your British tendencies, miss, but you can't hurry up the perfect winged eyeliner. Trust me, I wish you could," and she went back to looking at herself in the mirror, nose against the glass.

"I'll pretend I didn't just hear you call me British. You know Ireland's not the same island, right?" I knew she knew. But she took every opportunity to annoy me with this. "Okay, Sienna, your turn. What have you decided on?" I face my other best friend, hoping this one will save me and my punctuality preference.

"I'll take this comfy pair of leggings with the sweater I brought on and my vest."

Liv almost jumps at Sienna, winged liner forgotten. "You can't wear leggings! No one will wanna bang you with leggings on! I just had those there from the yoga session I did earlier."

"Well, too late! They're comfy." Sienna gives it one last tug to pull the leggings over her ankles, while Liv stares at her, mouth open. "We're just going to the Swing, Liv, I want to be warm and comfortable to sit around. I don't intend to make out with our former peers, I didn't have interest in any of them back then, and I surely don't have any interest now."

Liv continues staring at her until something crosses her face. She gasps. "Ahh, you sneaky little rat! What were you doing a couple of days ago in Providence? Why are you, all of a sudden, excited about going to the Clubhouse?" Liv looks at me as if I can read her mind and should be aware of what she's getting at.

"Pfffffftt! I don't know what you're on about. Tee, what are you g-"

"Not so fast, little rat! Go on, tell us all about it!" Liv cuts her mid-sentence.

"Oohh," I gasp, "Sienna! Are you dating someone?" I finally catch up to where Liv's mind's been for the last couple of minutes.

When she doesn't say anything, I continue, "S! Are you?"

She blushes, I can literally see her turning red from her toes to her hair roots. She squeaks a little, "No?"

"Is that a question? How would we know if *you*'re dating? Apparently, we're not worthy of your news," that came from Liv. She declared herself the queen of detecting when someone's had sex a long time ago, and I have full trust on her. Well, maybe had.

"Liv, I've told you to not annoy her. S, why didn't you share this news with us? I think what Liv was trying to say was, we're your best friends and thought you'd like to tell us these things. Help us understand."

She seems to consider this before letting herself fall on the bed, "Well, it's not like I didn't want to tell you. I just really didn't know how. It's new, and I'm not really dating anyone. Well, I don't think so anyway. It's complicated…" She deflates a little and I can see there's a whole lot to this story.

"Hmmm, do you want to talk about it now or would you rather wait-"

Liv interrupts me, "Wait? You want her to wait? For what? She needs to spill the beans now! Yesterday, even!"

"Liv, shut up, let me finish. S, would you rather wait for when you've had enough time to think about this and figure out if you are or not dating after all?"

"I guess so," she seems to debate the next words in her head, "I just don't have anything to share yet. I think that's it. I may have a little interest in someone, but I haven't even talked to him…"

This shocks Liv, "You haven't *talked* to him?? And how is that dating?"

"I never told you I was dating! You were the one who assumed I was. And stop rolling your eyes at me. I was going to say something the other night at Gallagher's but then…" She looks over in my direction but stares at the floor instead, "then he," she whispers, "showed up. I couldn't just talk about it then. I promise you'll both be the first ones to know when something happens. I may need your help anyway." She shrugs.

Liv seems to accept this. "Alright then. We'll be here to hear all about the sex you'll have once you have it! And for any tips you may need. Even though I recommend getting the entire thing, not just the tip." She winks and runs off to put her nose up to the mirror again and Sienna throws a pillow at her.

A good hour later, we're finally parking by the lake. I decided to steal Liv's black leather jacket that has a cardigan and a hood on the inside for extra warmth, and I paired it with the black skinny jeans I was already wearing and a plaid shirt. My knee-high brown boots give me an extra layer on my legs, and my head is wrapped with a dark red beanie.

"I'd forgotten how beautiful it is here at nightfall," I say to them, feeling taken aback by the million lights twinkling, the smell of wood burning and the crisp cold air. This area by the lake was a special one, I had spent some magical times here over the years. We would sit on the wooden deck chairs by the water, and let the conversation take us away from everyone else around us. Listening to the soft washing away of the water, undulating from the rare boat or two, that melody would always transport me to the quietest places of my mind, the safest ones. Sometimes, Knox would take advantage of that and ask me 'life questions', as he said it one day, such as, "If no one was listening to your answer, what would you say is your biggest dream?", or the one time we had been watching all the Marvel movies in order of release, "Why do you think they chose 3000? Why not 3001?" this one had made me laugh, and he looked at me dead serious and told me he wasn't kidding. We had to Google that one later because he wouldn't let it go. Me, I'd always liked the magic of just pondering on things for a while, and not have the answer instantly at the tip of your tongue. "What are we going to do when I get a scholarship and move away?" he had decided to ask one night only a couple of months into our relationship. That question wasn't Googled, nor did it get an answer that night... or ever.

"*Heeeeeeyy*, Matt! What's up?" I'm thrown into real time with Sienna greeting an old peer.

"Not much," he says, "just hanging around. What about you guys?" he faces me and Liv.

She's quick to answer, "Did you grow some more after we graduated? I don't remember you being this tall, little Matt."

He laughs at her, probably remembering how she used to be, no surprise there, she and her sassy mouth haven't changed. "I guess I did grow some more, Liv. It's nice to see you didn't change at all."

She curtsies at him, "My pleasure," she adds, which makes me roll my eyes and sigh.

"Hey, Matt, nice to see you here." I pull him in for a hug. We used to hang out a lot in our sophomore year, since I watched and waited for Knox and the team's practice to be done every day.

We make rounds saying hi to everyone we knew back in high school and to a few, new girlfriends and boyfriends some people brought. That's what you always want to see, happy people in happy relationships to remind you of how single you currently are. I don't think I could stand here to watch them all wrapped up in each other if it wasn't for the two beers I'd already had. I felt like I had a little buzz going on, so I could now continue hanging around all the couples without wanting to go drown in the lake.

"Damn, I feel like such a party pooper tonight", I tell Liv and Sienna when we make our way towards three available deck chairs.

"What? Why? I haven't seen you say anything wrong tonight," Sienna tells me.

"I know, but if you were in my head, you'd say otherwise" and with that, I take another swig of my beer and lay my head against the back of the chair.

"It's fine, guys, I'm fine. Don't look at me like that," they're both looking at me with their puppy eyes, "I just didn't think this would be the difficult part. Seeing everyone, most of them all happy and coupled up, but also being right here, the water, the moon, the fairy lights everywhere..." I sigh, "I just wasn't thinking about it all. I think I just pushed it away and thought I'd deal with the consequences when I got here, and alas, I am dealing with them now." I take another swig for good measure.

"Honey, we know," they exchange looks, communicating non-verbally, "Do you want us to go? We could go to Gallagher's and have fun there", Sienna suggests, while putting a comforting hand on my left knee.

"Nah, thanks, but not necessary!" I try to shake away the nostalgic memories, "I'm all good, I just needed to sit down for a bit. Do you wanna do me a favor and go get me another beer? I'm all done." I show them my bottle.

"Sure thing, hon, I'll get one for myself as well. Be right back!" Sienna seems too eager to have something useful to do.

"Hey," Liv taps my right arm, "are you sure you want to stay? I can find my next 'to-do' another night", she winks at me, "Besides, I think Matt looked like he could lay down for a bit, so no need to overstay our welcome, target was acquired!"

I laugh at her, "Liv, you can't talk like that all the time. If people hear you, they'll think you're discussing nuclear strategies and such."

She dismisses me with a wave of her hand, "Are you gonna be okay for a few minutes if I just go throw my shot quickly and remind Matt how much he wants me?"

"Sure thing, try not to spook him!", I yell at her but she's already snaking around people, her eyes locked on her target.

I laugh to myself and shake my head. She's always so positive, I don't think she knows the words 'I can't', what a wonder that must be, to live a life just believing you can, anything you want, because why not. I feel a little breeze and wrap Liv's coat tighter and turn around looking for Sienna and my beer.

I find her among some people, who I believe must be the theater crowd because there's a lot of nodding and gestures happening. I sigh, I think she'll be awhile.

I turn my head to the other side when I hear some shouts and a couple of claps, and I immediately regret my decision.

Knox's wearing dark jeans that seem to mold to his thick thighs and perfectly shaped butt, a plaid shirt with sleeves rolled up to his elbows, showcasing his tanned arms and watch on his right wrist. Ugh, I'm such a sucker for forearms and watches. Seems like a deadly combo. I can already feel my insides turning looking at him. It's almost as if he dressed just for me, targeting all my weak spots. The thick forearms, the watch, the plaid against dark jeans, his hair swooping to one side, and he didn't shave. I bet he smells delicious too, I imagine it travelling between the twenty feet separating us and my body trembles with his manly odor.

Our eyes meet through the crowd, but he's the first to look away this time.

Dreams and imagination shattered all around me, I get up and look for comfort next to Sienna and her group of theater aficionados.

"Hey, is everything okay?" she leans in and whispers to me.

"Yeah, he's just arrived though, and I wanted some emotional and physical support." I shrug. "Is that beer for me?"

"Yeah," she hands it to me while searching the crowd for him and when she sees him, she gives me a sympathetic look.

I try to smile at her, "It's okay", my voice nearly above a murmur.

Beyond seeing him move smoothly from group to group, saying his hellos to people he probably doesn't even remember, I *feel* him. I can sense his heavy presence, the closer he moves towards our group, the harder it gets to breathe. My chest is constricted and the beer I'm nursing doesn't make me looser as I'd hoped.

He moves again, coming right into our circle, and says "Hey, everyone, how are you guys doing?" He speaks like there's no weight on his chest, no awkwardness being here, a mere feet away from my presence. I'm just another schoolmate to him.

Sienna chirps up, "Ox! Hi!" she moves to hug him, "How is our town's superstar? How's Chi-town treating you?" She's always been able to make small talk, and it never felt like she was forcing anything, she's just great at making people feel at ease and like she truly wants to hear what they had to say.

"Oh, you know, windy." That gets a chuckle out of everyone present, but not me. I don't think I've been breathing for the last couple of minutes.

"Nah, it's going great, training's hard, but I'm where I'm supposed to be." I don't know if I imagined it or not, but I'm sure he looked at me for a split second when he said those last words.

Sienna flinches next to me, in a way so subtle only people who know her well would notice. She got the same meaning as me, 'Ouch, I'm sorry', she seems to say telepathically.

I dare to look up at him now, wanting to confront him and his words. I feel so small inside, but my brain wants me to fight and show him I don't give a flying duck about him being where he's *supposed* to be. In my head, I'm sticking my tongue out at him and repeating his words at him dramatically. 'Triona, get your act together now, you're not 5', my left brain scolds me.

"I'm gonna say hi to the rest of the gang, nice to see you again, guys." And with that, he leaves us and I'm suddenly aware of how cold it is. I zip up my jacket and pull the beanie on my head lower to cover my ears.

"Give us a moment, I need another." Sienna shows the group an empty bottle in her hand and pulls me to the side, making her way towards the coolers.

"Are you okay?" she asks when we've stepped away from everyone else.

"Sure thing" I say, looking defeated. She obviously doesn't believe me. I sigh. "He didn't even say hi to me, did you see that? I was there too, like Amy or Trent or whatever their names are, and he was just *there*. Like I was nobody." I feel a huge weight moving from my lower stomach to my throat. "S, he said he's where he's supposed to be…" I look down at my feet, tears pooling in my eyes. No, I won't cry here. It's humiliating enough I seem to be the only one thinking about the fact we hadn't seen each other in over 4 years. "Nothing to say to me", I whisper.

"Hon, let's go then. It's okay, we don't have to stay. I don't want to stay any longer." Sienna encourages.

I see through the corner of my eye someone approaching us and then, Liv is next to us. "Hey, what's up? Did you see him arrive? I was with Matt, I didn't notice, I'm so sorry, Tee", this seems to genuinely pain her.

"Yes, but it's fine, Liv. I was just telling Sienna that I'm ready to go home, but you guys will stay here. You'll enjoy your time with our old mates, and you will…um, well, I guess you'll enjoy Matt's company." That makes her crack a smile at me.

"Sure will!" then she looks momentarily concerned, "How are you gonna get home?"

"It's okay, I'll just walk. I need to clear my head before going to sleep."

I give them both a quick hug and I say my goodbyes.

When I arrive home a half hour later, I'm still seething. Who does he think he is to just plainly ignore me. It's not like we hooked up once or twice back in high school. I spent almost two and a half years of my life with him, loved him for nearly all that time and I'm sure he had better things to do than pretend to love me back for that time. So for him to come back now and pretend I don't exist is just plain rude. At least a quick hi, I don't know, a glance my way not to say 'I'm where I'm supposed to be', but more like 'Hey, we haven't seen each other in a while, and even though I have a different side piece on my arm every night, I still cherish that time we spent together, and hey, it's been 4-fucking-years, so maybe I'll apologize now for leaving you after making you love me more than life.' You know, something along those lines, I reckon.

"Ugh, stop living in your head, Triona, he has every right to do whatever he wants to and with whomever he wants to do it." I whisper out loud.

I change into my pajamas and snuggle in bed, getting that initial cold-sheet shiver until, slowly, warmth spreads around me and I close my eyes.

Living in the past has got to stop. I can't continue thinking about him and checking him up on every news media Chicago has to offer. I knew I had to finally move on, maybe start dating back in New Haven. I found a weekly singles night at a bar near the campus and I refused to go there because I like to believe my person and I would meet at a coffee shop, getting our orders mixed and our fingers lingering when we exchange them. Or we'd bump into each other at the entrance of the Ingalls Rink, not that I even enjoy hockey, but I love to sit around and gape at the building. Bottom line is, I never imagined it happening at a bar, on singles night, where everyone attending is there to meet a match. It feels forced… like I must find someone to plan out a future with. It's just too much pressure.

Knox and I had officially met on bonfire night a little over 7 years ago, and even though later he admitted he had seen me around school before, – we never had the same classes because of our 2-year gap - that night was the first time we actually talked. I was grabbing myself something to drink while everyone around us was cheerfully dancing and drunk, and the guys from the football team were playing around us. I had just chosen what to drink when I saw a football fly in my direction, and all I had time to do was duck and crouch to prevent it from slapping me across the face. In that same second, Knox jumped over to catch it and even though he didn't miss the ball, he didn't see me, so his right foot still kicked me in the shoulder when he was landing.

"Oh! Ouch!", I'd said while grabbing my right shoulder. The impact had pushed me down to falling fully on my butt.

"Oh, hey! I'm really sorry! Are you okay? Did I hurt you?" his eyes were everywhere, searching my face, looking over every part of me to find any damage done.

"You kicked me in the shoulder, jackass!" I yelled back at him. I don't know if the pain I felt was pure humiliation or if he'd dislocated my shoulder.

"Lemme see." Only then did I happen to notice his green, stormy eyes. He threw the ball back in the direction of his teammates and continued to look at me. "Can you move it?" he asked me while putting his right hand delicately on my shoulder.

"It's fine, I'm fine. You can go away now, player." Did I mention I used to hate football? Its players included. I had a foul mouth on me, well, still kind of do, but I can't compete with Liv these days.

He helped me up, as if I was a damsel in distress and couldn't very well use my own two legs to stand up, and instructed me "Move it around, so I can see if you've dislocated it."

Apparently, he didn't care that I had told him to leave. Players are definitely crazy, playing around in any season and not listening to what non-players had to tell them.

I moved my arm a bit, and it didn't hurt enough to be dislocated or torn. "Okay, you saw it now. I'm leaving. Try not to knock down any more girls while you're at it, player."

Only then he seemed to stop worrying about my shoulder and looked at me and chuckled, 'I'm Ox... the player", he added, and extended his hand to me, "nice to meet you."

What were we? 40? Who shook hands in high school? Jesus.

"Okay. Bye now." And I went back to find Liv and Sienna among the crowd, leaving him and his handshake.

But of course he liked the chase, otherwise he wouldn't be so happy to run around a football and other players half of his life, so he found me again that night. And I let him sit next to me, and by the end of the night, he had me genuinely laughing with him.

Tut-tut. What have I told you, brain? Stop going to places you'll regret before you're able to say 'I told you so'.

I closed my eyes and let the images of fire sparkling, fairy lights and his scent drift me to sleep.

Clink.

Silence.

Clink.

I rustle awake.

Clink.

I don't make a move. What's that noise. Did I leave the tap open in the bathroom?

Silence.

Clink. Clink.

My heart starts hammering against my rib cage. I stop breathing.

Clink.

I recognized that sound now. I hadn't heard it a long, long time, but I knew what it was now.

I push my blanket to my feet, lightly drop my feet to the floor and take four quiet steps towards my window.

The street is lit up with all the Christmas lights from every one of my parents' neighbors' homes, so I can see outside clearly.

He bends over, grabbing another little pebble, but stops before throwing it against my window, seeing me.

There he was.

Again.

8.

Knox climbs up the wide Willow Oak like he's done many times before and reaches the roof that connects to my now, open window.

"Oxie, have you forgotten how much I dislike rom-com clichés?" I tease him for his habit of calling for me this way since I was 16. It's not like phones haven't been invented or something.

"Have *you* forgotten how much I dislike when you call me Oxie?" he shoots back, pushing me aside the window so he can step inside, jumping over my window seat. He probably still remembers how much I despise wearing shoes in the house and the thought of putting them anywhere near my bed or my beloved window seat would just drive me bonkers.

A silence falls, blanketing us in the darkness. I can hear him swallow. My breathing accelerating. His breathing. But all around us, this heavy silence rings in my ears making me feel like I'm running a high fever all of a sudden.

Then, noise.

I hear rustling and the familiar creak of my window closing, then the latch clicking against the cold metal.

He faces me again, I can see his shape only lit by the Christmas lights outside. "Hi", he says matter-of-factly.

He sounds so easy-going, not a single trace of faltering in his voice.

"Um-hi", I say, trying to even my voice as much as I can. "Let me hit the light." I take the few steps towards my bedside table and switch on that lamp. Soft lighting is probably the best lighting solution for whatever this will be.

"Is this awkward? I feel this is awkward", he shrugs in front of me, sliding both hands into his jeans' pockets.

I sit on the edge of my bed with my left leg under me. I make a motion for him to sit down on the window seat.

"We haven't seen each other in a long time… I guess it's bound to be a little awkward, don't you think?" I tell him, but speaking more to myself trying to calm my nerves more than I am talking to him.

"I guess so… We haven't seen each other in a couple of hours, though. It hasn't been that long", he smirks, trying to lighten the mood.

I suddenly realize I'm not wearing a bra under my pajama shirt, so I get up and reach inside my closet to find a warm fleece jacket to put on. I sit down on my bed again and look towards him.

"You didn't talk to me, Knox. Not a word in the two times you've seen me in the last few days. What are you doing here now?"

He looks away, and I watch his Adam's apple throb, "I just wanted to talk to you, Triona. I'm sorry about before, but I just didn't expect you to be in town so early, or not at all even, and it caught me off guard."

"Right. That was at the pub." I try to let him off the hook that one time, "But what about tonight? You said hi to Sienna and everyone around. I know you saw me… You looked at me. So, what's your explanation for that one? Because for sure you'd know I was also attending, right? Matt was in my class, and he was the one throwing the party tonight", I manage to say it all without taking a breath.

It takes him a few moments to reply, "I honestly don't have a good enough reason. I was just being a jackass," he shrugs, "Wanted to see if you'd react, say something to me," he adds a second later, "but you didn't."

"Hmmm. I get that," I sigh, "This *is* awkward."

That gets a laugh out of him. "Safe ground", he lifts his hands up, signaling a truce, "How's everything? How are your parents?"

I smile. "They're doing great. You know, mom still gives dad crap about his cooking, and he still loves it when she does." It's impossible not to smile at how easy my parents' relationship seems to be. "They're just so happy, you know. Kinda crazy to think they've been together for over 25 years."

He seems to get uncomfortable with something. "Yeah… that is a really long time." He ponders for a few seconds and then asks, "How's New Haven treating you?"

I eye him curiously now, "Well. A lot of studying has been done in New Haven, but it's treating me well. I got an internship lined up for the summer, so I'm thrilled about that. How's Chicago?" I attempt to ask. I'm not sure if this is still 'safe ground' as he first suggested.

"That's great news, congrats, Ina! I'm sure you're gonna kill it. And Chicago's great too. Living the dream, you know…" So much said in such a few words. For starters, he called me Ina. I don't even know if he realized he'd said it, but I'm gonna go with force of habit… Then, he said he's living his dream, which I happen to know is true. It's slightly disconcerting to hear it nonetheless, but I get it. He went through a lot to get to where he's at now, of course he's happy and thriving.

He notices my silence and the time we spent together doesn't seem to have vanished completely because he surprises me by saying, "Are you overthinking everything just now?" he waits for a couple beats before adding, "Tee, I had to say hi. It's been forever and we've both moved on. We have different lives in different states. I thought I could at least be cordial and find out how you're doing and what's new. My first reactions weren't a prime example of that, but I promise I'm here with the best intentions and all I really wanted was to catch up." He proceeds to remove his shoes and sit on the floor, "Is that okay with you?"

I lack for words that could express how I'm feeling right now, however, he's right. Again. It's been a long time and he has certainly moved on, I've seen the pictures online, so I think it's not a bad idea if we can just catch up and be okay around each other. Our town is not that big and we're bound to meet each other over the years. Our parents still live here, after all.

"Ehm, yeah, you're right." I shake my head, peeling all negative thoughts away along with it, "You're absolutely right. It has been a significantly large amount of time, and we should be able to be around each other. So, catch me up! I'm ready to be all caught up." I slide down onto the floor in front of him, my back against my bed frame.

"Umm, let me think…", he says to me clearly thinking about what to say, "How much do you know?"

"Nothing", I lie.

His eyes move up towards mine, and he clears his throat. "Right. Well, we have practice every day that there's not a game and I've pretty much been kicking ass," he smiles, "I feel like I should work more than I do because I see my teammates frustrated with the game, but I never feel that way. I feel like this is really where I'm supposed to be and when you have that awareness, all else falls into place and you feel like you're just cruising in life, you know what I mean?" His words knock the breath out of my chest. *'No'*, I want to shout, *I don't know what you mean.* I've been trying to cruise for 4 years and the closest I got to it was during finals' week in my first year when I didn't sleep nor eat for that amount of time, but I probably only felt like I was cruising because my head was too light from not eating and my body felt like it was floating.

But instead, I say, "Yeah, I think I do. That's exactly how I feel back in New Haven." I lie through my teeth, "I'm beyond ecstatic about my internship and can't wait for the summertime."

"Tell me more about it", he nudges my foot with his when I don't continue.

"I don't have much to say about it yet, it hasn't started," I shrug.

"But tell me how you got it. How you chose it. I'm sure there was a pretty thorough pros and cons list to help you make a decision, wasn't there?" he teases.

"Umm…no, I don't believe there was," but we both end up laughing at my words. "Okay, okay, there was maybe a tiny-wee list. However, I only had to make one this time because I got accepted into three agencies and they all had its advantages. I wanted to make sure I ended up choosing the right one."

"And did you?"

There's no doubt in my voice this time, "Abso-freakin-lutely! They're amazing there! The agency is run by women, and I'll be working alongside Lindsay Milokovski, can you believe it? Lindsay-all-powerful-better-than-Thor-Milokovski!!" I hear myself screech and realize I'm a little too excited for 3am, so I clear my throat and whisper, "I'm just so elated with this opportunity. I hope I won't fuck it up."

"I'm sure you won't, Ina. And congrats! I don't know who Lindsay, better than Thor, *ha?*, Milokovski is, but I'm sure she's a big deal for you to be so crazy happy," he pauses mulling over his words, "I'm happy for you too, Ina. You deserve it."

My heart clenches around those selected words. Is this his way of letting me know that he still cares, even though his dream was bigger than our relationship, than us?

"Are you dating anyone?" he pulls me away from my thoughts.

"Wh-what? Why?" I just don't see how the conversation turned in this direction. Talking about an architectural goddess doesn't really scream dating to me, or maybe it does? Her buildings are definitely elegant, sexy and make you want to stare at them for hours on end. Maybe that's why he made that connection?

"Just catching up, Triona," he says, indifferently.

"Ohh…Ummm…", what should I tell him, what should I say… "I mean, not right now, no. Yeah. I'm not dating right now." I nod my head, accepting what I just said. It's not a lie, I am not dating at the moment, he never asked about if I've dated. Totally different tense.

"Right", his eyes meander around my room, landing on different parts of my life. Photos from the past I keep on a corkboard hanging on the wall. Photos he's in. Mementos from high school are also spread on different walls. An old poster of Channing Tatum peeking from behind a pile of laundry I haven't folded yet.

"What about you?" I interrupt his curiosity, "Are you dating?"

He faces me, not a glimpse of a smile to be found, "No."

That's it? No? I'm well aware he's been dating. I've seen it all on the online photos and news. Does he truly believe I know nothing about him? I mean, how could I not? He's a star back here, famous around the nation amongst those who know a thing or two about football, and we dated. He was my whole world… How would I *not* know?

"Wow, I didn't know we started lying to each other now," I can't stop the words from leaving my mouth.

"What? Why are you saying that?" he seems confused.

"I know you're dating!" my arms are crossed on my chest now, I'm huffing, and all I have left to do is pout and say I won't go out unless I'm allowed to put my pink fluffy dress on. 'Three-year-old' suits me.

"What are you saying?" he is looking at me like I'm crazy, "How would you know if I'm dating or not? You're not in my life anymore."

That does it. I take a visible sharp breath, clearly hurt with his words.

"I didn't mean it like that, Ina", he moves closer and takes my hand in his. "You're in my life. You always have been. You know that. But why do you think I'm lying? Why would I lie to you now?", his eyes are pleading mine now.

"It's okay, Knox, you just took me by surprise, that's all," I free my hands from his, "But of course you're right, I wouldn't know. And I am not in your life anymore. That's true as well."

I stand up, not letting him touch me any longer. "I'm going downstairs to make myself a cup of tea. You can use the front door to leave."

I open my bedroom door and go down the stairs without taking a look behind me to see if he's following.

9.

A couple of minutes later, just when I was starting to believe he had left through my bedroom window again, he shows up in the kitchen. I can hear him behind me, moving towards my right, opening the cupboard above the coffee machine to retrieve some tea bags. "Are you in the mood for black or green?", he veers toward me to show me what he's found in the cupboard.

"Green."

Then, remembering my manners, I add, "Thank you."

He smiles, "You're welcome. I'll have some green too." So he goes over to the other side and gets us two mugs, picking my favorite one, a tall black one with speckles of gold, resembling the night sky.

"I know you'd want this one. I haven't met anyone else who has such a specific liking for mugs. You know the tea will taste all the same, right?" it's not only the smirk on his face that tells me he's teasing me because we used to have this conversation almost every morning when I would go over to his parents' house to make him breakfast after he got injured during that touchdown, but I still can't help my answer.

"It surely doesn't taste the same! The mug chosen is pure magic and will dictate how amazing your coffee or tea turns out. And why would I risk drinking anything from an *un*-magical mug, only to have my whole day ruined?"

Is the three-year-old making a comeback?

He laughs, "I know, Tee, I'm just grilling you. I remember how special your mugs have to be. Here." He hands me my night sky mug, "I really meant it. You are in my life. Hell, this whole town is in my life", he pushes my shoulder as if to play with me, "I just don't want you to think I'm lying to you. I really am not dating, why did you believe otherwise?"

"I lied before", I admit to him, "I've seen you in the press, and I've seen the photos of the many, many women you're *not* dating."

"Er-right," he states matter-of-factly, "You've seen photos of me with a few different women that I have to take to events. Is that it?"

"Well, I don't know what events or whatever. All I'm saying is, I have seen you date. So, you *were* lying to me," he doesn't miss how strained my voice gets throwing these words back at him.

"Triona, I really wouldn't consider taking a woman with me to an event '*dating*'", he uses his index and middle finger around the word dating.

"Right." I uncross my arms that seem to have found their way against my chest again, blocking this conversation from reaching my heart. And because I can't help myself, I add, "So what would you consider dating? Please enlighten me", the kettle makes its screeching noise and I start pouring tea into both mugs.

"I don't know. Well, for starters, *if* I'm dating someone, I'll take them out to dinner. I'll probably get laid. Oh, and I most certainly wouldn't be obliged per my contract terms to be accompanied to my team events."

I feel his eyes following my movements, from mug to mug, to placing the kettle on the counter before handing him his mug.

"Ooh!" he has to take a date to events… Hmm, that's new information I didn't read in any news articles. "Er… Right. A date is usually a tad bit more romantic, isn't it?" I try to come up with something to say to him.

"Why, yes, it is, Tee", even though he hides his face by bringing his mug up to his lips to blow on the hot liquid inside, I still see his smirk. "And even though the women I bring to these things are, unquestionably, gorgeous, I really hate mixing business with pleasure. If I go out on a date, I don't want to get my pictures taken or for the whole world to know about my personal life."

"Sure, sure. Makes sense, I guess." I start slurping away on my tea to create a distraction within myself. The thoughts that have been invading my quiet moments ever since stepping foot back in town are not only making me question some past decisions, but also distracting me from my own strength, self-love and kindness. I don't dwell on others' happiness, whether they were my boyfriend or not. I have to keep reminding myself that his actions shouldn't matter, he has moved on, and I should be happy for his promising future, professional and otherwise.

He's still studying me after my inner turmoil fades away, and wanting to push those crippling feelings away, I say, "Are you still going to physical therapy?"

I honestly couldn't think of anything else to say, but those words just don't make a lot of sense, considering it's been years since he got hurt.

He laughs at my question, crosses his arms around his chest and tucks each hand under his bicep before saying, "You'd think physical therapy is only for injuries, but that's actually a great question, because I still see a therapist every week."

I sit up on the kitchen counter, bringing my mug closer, "Why's that?"

"I just want to make sure everything's working how it's supposed to, you know?" before I could even nod my head, he continues, "I think it really got me when I got injured. I was really in a dark cloud during that time…" he glances my way, following the mug touching my lips and down towards my throat when I swallow. "I'm sure you remember…"

He moves around the island, putting some more distance between us, and gulps down some tea as if it was cold water.

I can't deny the emotions that overwhelm me when he mentions that time. We spent so much time together, I wanted to make sure he was happy and comfortable. I wanted to be the bright light guiding him towards the exit I knew he was so desperate to find. Finding out physical therapy wouldn't be enough almost killed him. I think he was really scared of having to get surgery so young. And I worked really hard to keep up with schoolwork, from the moment I would leave his home at night and in the early mornings before going to school. I had been consumed by him, I saw him almost 12 hours every day, at school and then at his place. I knew every single beauty mark on his body, the way his pupils dilated when he was really focused on something, the tiny flashes of pain across his forehead during his physical therapy sessions and all the places he was ticklish. I got to know him inside out. His routine, his food preferences, his propensity to waste water in the shower, and his kind heart. The truth is, if I hadn't been in love with him before that treacherous night, I would have completely fallen in love with him throughout those months before the summer.

No one could escape Knox Noah's charm.

He was made for loving.

Turning my face up towards him, I whisper, "I remember, Ox, I'll always remember."

I see his jaw muscles contract at my words, and his Adam's apple bobs. He slowly turns to face me again, the intensity in his eyes hitting me like a sound wave. My whole body heats up looking at him, and I lick my lips, trying to wet them. He watches me and I can see his muscles tense up underneath his shirt.

I feel like I'm spiraling out of control and soon I won't be able to escape what's happening. I clear my throat and trying to stop whatever's happening, ask, "So, what's your favorite part about Chicago? Have you explored the city a lot?" I take that opportunity to drink some more of my tea, which does nothing to cool me down, but helps with the dryness in my mouth.

That seems to break his intensity, and he lifts the mug to his lips and takes a couple of sips before answering, "Yeah, I've explored a bit. It's difficult when you have practice and games every day, but during the off-season when I'm in town, I've been able to explore a bit," he takes another sip, giving him time to think about his next words, "Hmm… I don't know what's my favorite part, I think I have a few favorites to be honest." He stops again to drink some more, I imagine, but he surprises me by saying, "I show you around if you're ever in town."

I tease him, "Why, superstar Knox Noah, out and about in Chicago, in plain daylight? Do you think that would be safe?", I make a serious face, "We wouldn't even be able to take two steps outside, and we'd swarmed by all your fans!" I hide my smile behind my mug.

"I have ways, you know… I won't say I've been grocery shopping recently, but I definitely go out and there are no fans blocking my path, Ina…" I stare at him, my eyebrows lifted. "Okay, okay, maybe there's a fan or two from time to time", he assumes defeat by raising his hands chest-height.

I laugh, "I'm sure there are a few more than just two, but I believe you. You can definitely give me a tour if I'm ever in Chicago again."

I wince at my words as soon as I feel them leave my lips.

"Again?" he inquires, "When have you ever been in Chicago? I don't remember you mentioning that when we were together."

I jump from the counter wanting to put even more distance between us, and while rinsing my mug in the sink, I say, "Oh, I went there just for a couple of days a few years ago. It was a quick trip."

He's behind me before I know it. "Ina, when?" his eyes search mine and his jaw is locked tight.

"I really can't remember now. A few years ago…", I try to step around him because I need space. I can feel my lungs constrict by how close he is, and I could never admit to him I was still waiting around for him, almost a year after he left me.

He grabs my forearm, "Ina, tell me… when?" he's pleading me now, I can see from his body language how much he wants to know this information. I just don't know why that would even matter right now.

"It doesn't matter, Knox." I let myself loose from his touch. "I've told you, I can't remember when exactly," I give him a little more, hoping this will shut him up, "I was in my first year, it was spring. I travelled a bit. That's all."

He's looking at me like I've just slapped him. I can see how upset he is, but I just don't understand why he has a reason to feel this way.

"Knox, I don't see why this matters. I wanted a weekend away from Connecticut."

"Triona, I think that a 14-hour-drive is a little too much for someone who wants a *'weekend'* away," he mocks by making air quotes on weekend. "You could have gone to New York. Boston. Cleveland even!"

"Okay, okay, Knox, I see your geographical skills are top-notch. Glad to see our school system didn't fail you. I still don't see any relevance to this." I shake my hands, trying to keep my voice down. He won't let me put this topic to rest.

"You don't see *why* this is important?!" He starts pacing across my parents' kitchen. "Triona, why wouldn't it be? I'm *there*! I was there", he stops to look at me and takes two steps towards me, eating away our distance in under one second.

I'm stuck in a corner now, against the cabinets.

I can feel his breath when he asks, "Did you go there for me, Ina? Did you go to Chicago to see me?"

I can hear the hope in his voice. I can feel his heart beating so quickly that his veins are jumping out of his skin. I can taste my happiness so close. I can almost touch it. But just one thought makes it all crash around me, and I'm back in this kitchen, a few years too late, with someone in front of me who I do not know anymore, someone who used to be my whole heart, but I can't let him in again, so I just say "No."

He exhales all the hope he had, disappointment flares his entire face, and he leaves me in the corner.

A raw breeze washes my body, an immediate bubbling of emotion crushes over me and I sob for what feels like hours, sitting empty on the cold tiles. Baby put herself in the corner this time.

10.

After twisting and turning in bed for a couple of hours, I can finally see daylight peeking through my window. It always amazes me how light can wash away the more negative feelings, it makes me feel like it gives me a new try at things, or a new perspective. The darkness has always enhanced the negative feelings and overthinking for me. So, seeing the daylight slowly caressing my bedroom, I decide it's time to put my tears away and take a mildly cold shower to wake me up properly.

I'd go for a run, but my body feels like it would need extra stretching today, and one thing I hate almost as much as the darkness is stretching.

Once the water hits me, I can feel my skin tighten and heart beating fast. There aren't many things that quite work as a shock to the system as a cold shower. The events from last night almost leave my mind entirely, but you know what they say about realizing you're no longer thinking of something, that thing comes crawling back to your thoughts just as quickly.

I figure most people wouldn't expect a high school couple to be together forever. I was of that opinion too, until I met Knox. I truly believed we would make it work. We went through quite a few bumps that could easily overwhelm anyone, let alone a teenager. When he got hurt that February, I had never seen a human being suffer as much, nor had I ever experienced such strong feelings of hopelessness. It was a dark time for both of us. I wanted to help, but felt like I couldn't and Knox, he just couldn't see a way out. When we finally made our way out of the darkness together, I truly believed nothing else could stop us. I loved him with a kind of love that would make poets envious and lyricists eager to put it on paper.

I tried to fight for that love before he even left for Chicago, it took up all my mental and physical energy. He heard from the University of Chicago 10 months after his surgery. I remember it was a hot, summer afternoon in June, and we were lying in bed watching a movie when he got a phone call. They told him they wanted to offer him a full-ride but he wouldn't be able to start the school year as normal, but had to wait for the second semester in January of the following year. From that June afternoon until he left 7 months later, I laid out maps, wrote pros and cons lists, read romance books, anything that could help me figure it out. I wanted, I needed to find a way for us to work long distance. I still had my senior year to get through and he would be too far away for weekend trips.

But every now and then, feelings of doubt assaulted me every single second of every day. Was it supposed to be this hard? Hadn't Rory and Jess just found a way, even with an entire town against them? And we had, what, a few hundred miles between us. Wasn't love supposed to conquer it all?

That's what I believed in, anyway. I tried to push those thoughts away, hit them off like Nadal on the court, but eventually, even the pro athletes need a break. I let it all consume me, devour my weakness - and in the end, I convinced myself that not trying was for the best.

I leave my room feeling restless and annoyed with myself. The cold shower hadn't helped at all. When I reach downstairs, my parents are already having breakfast.

"Morning, pa," I kiss him on the cheek, "Morning, ma," also kissing her on the cheek. "It looks like we're having the breakfast of champions over here. Do we still have some more black pudding?" I ask, eyeing the pan.

"Of course we do, tootsie. We made extra for you," he hands me a plate filled to the edges with beans, a couple of hash browns and a few slices of black pudding. "I'll toast you some bread too."

"You're up early," my mom says, "Do you have any plans this morning?"

I can see her eyeing me curiously, and I wonder if she heard anything last night. She's not the heaviest sleeper. "Nope!" I try to muster up some enthusiasm, "I just woke up and felt like enjoying the day. I might do some last-minute shopping in town."

My dad hands me some toast and we all continue enjoying our breakfast.

"Oh, I almost forgot to tell you", my mom says to my dad, tapping him on the wrist calling his attention. "We might have to call the Johnsons again. I woke up last night with some noise coming from the outside of the house. I think Cinnamon was up on the roof again." I don't miss the quick side eye she gives me. I knew she must have heard us. This woman is the true definition of an Irish mom, just knows everything that happens in her house, for fuck's sake.

I roll my eyes at her, "Mom, I'm well aware you know that cat has seen better days and wasn't climbing up our house."

She feigns shock. "How am *I* supposed to know that? It's not my cat! And what are you on about? *Who* else could it be?" She raises her eyebrows and puts a hand to her chest. If I hadn't known her my whole life, I would believe her innocence, but I know better. My dad does too.

He faces me and asks, "What's happening, mo stór?" then turning to my mom, "Why are you grilling her?"

I can see my mom considering staying in character for a second, but she apparently changes her mind, "She knows what I'm talking about." She looks at me, "No cat would let us know before climbing up our window, now, would they?"

I drop my fork and knife on my plate and cross my arms, "I'm an adult, mom, I can have whomever I want in my room, during the day or at night." Did I just recede 8 years and became a teenager in 5 seconds flat? *Sure.* But my whole interaction with Knox last night left me feeling easily triggered and reluctant to share what happened with other people.

"Hon, of course you can have anyone you want up in your room," she says, her voice sincere, "Just tell Knox to use the front door next time." With that, she gives me the biggest grin.

"Knox was here last night?" this is my dad asking, ever the biggest fan. "Why didn't you wake me up?"

You can't honestly make up my parents. They've always been too involved in my life, and have always loved Knox. He was a member of our family for a while, and it was hard on my parents when we went our separate ways, probably mostly because of how it affected me. That's another reason why it's been hard for me to come back home. I not only have to see all our former favorite places, but I also have to hear everyone in town talk about him, and my parents still bombard me with questions to this day.

"Dad, it was 3am. I wasn't waking anyone up. He only stayed for a while, anyway. I was tired and wanted to go to bed." I say trying to make a complex situation sound a lot simpler. To change topics, I add, "How many people are you expecting for lunch at the pub tomorrow?"

It works like a charm, "Oh, everyone in town for sure!" my dad beams.

Whenever my dad started talking about Christmas Eve and the infamous lunch at the pub that the whole town attended every year, there was no stopping him. Knox had officially left the conversation.

I breathed a sigh of relief. I could now enjoy my black pudding in peace.

It still didn't escape me when my mom eyed me with a little smirk on her face, and I knew she had hit a nerve on purpose.

When I arrived downtown, the stores were still closed, so I went to the corner shop for a black coffee and glazed doughnut. I had so much to get done today, I couldn't believe I'd left this many gifts to be purchased so last minute. I'm usually pretty good at being ready for Christmas and buy all my gifts months in advance. I even forget what I got people because I plan it so far ahead. But this year, life flew by, and the nervousness of coming back home made it so I just could not focus on anything other than making it here and surviving until the new year.

Once I'm sitting down with my piping hot coffee, I grab my notebook and start making a list of all the people I still have to buy presents for. Dad, for one, who is always the easiest one to shop for because he absolutely loves anything I can get him. I might go for a nice pair of comfortable shoes since he's been complaining about his lower back after standing for too long at the pub. Mom is the next one on my list because I feel like what I got her the other day might not be enough, but I know just the store to get her something. I'll probably end up buying her a box of tea tasting or a simple necklace from the jewelry store. She always loves putting on a dainty necklace when she feels like dressing up a little, and it's been a tradition of ours that I'm the one who gets her new jewelry every year for Mother's Day or her birthday. This year, I didn't for either, so Christmas it is. I'd already got presents for Liv and Sienna back in New Haven, so I just need to find a couple more for my parents' neighbors, Nico at the pub, whom I've known since I was 11, and a couple more for my cousins who I'm seeing tomorrow night.

I'll also keep an eye out for some generic presents I can find, maybe a couple of chocolate boxes that I'll wrap up and offer someone I might see in town unexpectedly. It was my dad who used to do it this for many years. He always bought a few boxes of chocolates, maybe a couple bottles of wine, because he always said that you never know who'll be stopping by around the holidays and you better be prepared with something because they'll bring you a present as well. I never thought much of it as a kid, I used to find it such a weird perspective to have, but I do see his point now and I've been doing the same for the last couple of years.

An hour or so later, when I'm finally shopping around town, I'm window shopping at a local boutique that sells every knickknack you could think of. In the bottom corner, I spot something that immediately brings a smile to my face. The Mystery Machine van from Scooby-Doo. It's a toy van that probably fits the palm of my hand and before I know it, my feet are taking me towards the door.

I make my way around the store, forcing my body to move past the window and towards other items that could be gift worthy. I find a cute plushie in the shape of an owl that reminds me of Sienna, and I grab it, even though I already have her present. And I find myself by the window again, where that blue and orange jumps at me amongst a dozen other items.

I don't know if I'll talk to him again after what happened last night, and I don't know if I'll ever have the guts to actually give it to him, but I decide against my better judgement and the cashier is ringing up my two items before I have time to change my mind again.

"Would you like me to wrap these up for you?" the young guy asks me.

Pulled into reality, I smile up at him and tell him, "No, thank you, I'll just do it myself."

I'm leaving the store and the bag with the van is burning my hand. I close my eyes and take a deep breath, there is no point in worrying about it now. I bought it and if the situation presents itself, I'll give it to him. It doesn't even have to mean anything, it's just a memory shared between former friends. *And lovers*, my brain tuts at me.

I roll my eyes at my own thoughts. It's done. I can even keep for myself, I convince myself. Yeah, I can just take it back with me to New Haven.

11.

Tomorrow's Christmas' day and as every year, the day before, the pub hosts its Christmas' eve luncheon, to which everyone in town shows up for. It's the most magical day of the year, and I had missed being here, celebrating with my hometown. Stepping into Gallagher's, I am immediately welcomed with the aroma of roast and gravy in the air. My parents love sprucing up the pub for the Christmas' luncheon even more than they do in December, and I see this year is no different. Everywhere I look, wreathes hang from the wooden poles, warm-white fairy lights cascade from the ceiling against the dark-toned walls, and a large Christmas tree is set up at the back, illuminated in reds and greens with ornaments that town people have brought over the years. My mom loves collecting special baubles that remind her of people or places she's visited. Their tree at home is also wrapped with unique ornaments she buys at different antique shops. Every chance I get, I also love finding out new ones to surprise her.

The pub is just as packed as I remember from every Christmas spent here. You barely have empty floor space to move around, but the room is filled with laughter and buzzing chatter that resonates across the pub.

I'm trying to help my parents with orders, racing from booth to booth with plates brimming with the delicious meal my dad made. Pints of beer are also flowing towards different tables and people who are standing around waiting for a place to sit. I think most people in town love my parents, but more than that, they could not pass up an opportunity to see everyone come together one day a year. This is the time to see old friends, neighbors and to hear all the latest gossip. Miss Patty is here somewhere, no doubt with an army of people who are dying to find out who shouted at whom at the supermarket, or who's been sleeping with whose son. I just hope no one is gossiping about me and the reasons why I didn't show my face around here for a while. Besides not being anybody's business, I hate knowing I'm in a room full of people questioning my motives and commenting on my behavior as a good daughter. If I was a pro-athlete, I'm sure no one would wonder why I couldn't make it home for special occasions, but old me, being a student, it becomes an affair of trepidation for those who are not even involved. My parents understood. Hell, they wanted me to focus on my studies, and they still managed to come see me a few times over the years when my dad would agree to close down the pub for a few days. It's not like I hadn't seen them in 4 years, and we FaceTime every day when I'm up in New Haven. It's the 21st century, children are allowed to move to other parts of the country. Not that anyone was asking *me*, but I didn't feel guilty about my decisions. I had decided it would have been too harsh for me to come back because of all the memories, so I hadn't.

"Hi Triona, look at you all grown up! How are you, darling?" Mr. Logan stops me when I sprint by his table.

"Merry Christmas, Mr. Logan!" I give him a quick, tight hug, "You look younger every day. Tell a girl what's your secret!" I smile wide at him.

"Oh, you flatter me, dear. Don't waste those compliments on an old person. And you look just as young as the last time I saw you!" he pats my arm.

"I won't say I don't believe you, I'll take that compliment anytime, Mr. Logan. Even though I have to say, I feel like I've aged a couple of decades with all the work I've had to do at college."

"But it'll all pay off eventually. Learning opens your mind to reasoning and your eyes to new worlds that a town like ours, as special as it may be, would never be able to offer you," he leans closer to me as if he was sharing a secret.

Mr. Logan, or Todd for his peers, was a history teacher at our high school and he had been my teacher before he retired. My parents told me he was now in charge of the History Club that got together every Tuesday in the town's public center. I could easily see it, as he had never been one for sitting idly while others did something. He was always the first volunteer for organizing school events and field trips, even in his early 60s.

"I have to disagree with you, Mr. Logan", I tell him, "I learned a lot during my time here and I would not change a thing", then I lean over his table, placing my left hand around my mouth and add, "Well, maybe a thing or two." I wink at him, and we both giggle like two fearless children after being told not to do something and still doing it.

"I have to get some more meals to hungry town people, Mr. Logan, but it was lovely seeing you again. I'll be sure to stop by your History Club next time I'm around." I notice how bright his eyes get hearing me, and I make a mental note to actually attend one of his events.

After a few more rounds of clearing plates off people's tables and serving four full trays of pints, I finally get off my feet and inhale a few roast potatoes with a heavy side of gravy.

"I don't think you're supposed to eat that fast, Tee. Isn't your stomach going to hurt after?" Sienna is staring at me gorging this food.

"What?", I ask her between bites.

"Let her be. She'll wash it down with a beer later.", Liv brushes it off.

My best friends arrived early at the pub to score the best table next to the Christmas tree. They know it's my favorite spot because it's also right under a speaker, and you can hear Bublé from here. Some wouldn't understand why my parents even bother with Christmas music, but what they don't know is that my dad also has a speaker in his kitchen and loves listening to music while cooking. You might not hear the music over the chatter and amusement, but he does; and so do we, with the best seats in the house.

When I'm finally down to my last potato, I say with my mouth still full, "Are you guys excited about spending tonight with your families? I feel like this is the first Christmas I can actually breathe again. I didn't realize how much it had impacted me to spend it not here in town. With you guys and with my parents. I think I might've even missed Miss Patty." Right on cue, I hear her boisterous laughter.

Liv puts her arm around me in a rare show of affection and shouts, "We've missed you too, tootsie!" she's laughing now, knowing how much I hate they use my dad's nickname for me from when I was a child.

Sienna has tears in her eyes, "Tee, we truly missed you. And I still haven't forgiven you guys for leaving me behind and going off on your life adventures without me."

I move over to her side and hug her tightly, "S, we love you. We didn't leave you because we wanted to. We're gonna have a lot of fun in the next few days and then we'll promise to visit each other once every other month. Deal?"

I offer them my pinky. We twirl our three pinkies together and make a deal that I hope we can all keep, as I have missed them terribly, especially in this last year of college with too many projects to finish.

I should have known from past experience that, in this town, I keep getting blindsided when I least expect it. I'm behind the counter, helping Nico serve pints and whiskeys, when I feel the air change. I look in the direction of the door, and sure enough, above all the heads, I see him. Though I knew his parents would be coming in, as they've been attending the luncheon for as long as my parents have done it, I'm still a little surprised to see him here.

My mind travels back to the Christmas luncheon a couple of months after we officially met at the bonfire night and how nervous I had been that morning. I probably changed outfits five times before deciding I'd rather be comfortable since I would be working long hours. I had put on brown gingham pants, a white t-shirt tucked into them and a pair of Nike sneakers. I had only brushed my hair but added a reindeer headpiece to remove my bangs from my face and layered a bright red lipstick that I had hoped wouldn't be all over my teeth every time I opened my mouth. Working at the pub could be exhausting, but the Christmas luncheon was on a level of its own, and I always felt like I needed to be underdressed to not overheat. One year, I literally wore denim shorts and flip-flops because I'd had enough of sweating through my shirts, but that had been a terrible idea since my feet smelled more of beer than the pub at the end of game night.

That day, he had come in earlier than his parents and we found a corner near the back to chat for a bit before I had to get back to waitressing' duties. As soon as I'd seen him, I felt like I could have fainted right there and then. Our conversations were still a little awkward, mostly because of me, though. Whenever I had feelings for somebody, my inner superhero goddess would bail on me just as quickly as two horny teenagers undressing in front of each other for the first time. I still tried to act cool and collected around him, but he would surprise me with random facts he knew, or questions about life that I would only dare thinking in my head, and I would be completely speechless and in awe of the person he was. It was hard not to fall utterly in love with him in a short amount of time. He made me want to open up even more and allow myself to explore whatever I felt like. He was so brilliantly himself that I just couldn't look away.

"Hey, Triona!" I snap back into present day and look at Nico, "Are you still here?" he moves behind me and grabs a bottle of whiskey, "You scared me for a second, thought we'd lost you." He fills up three round, short glasses and slides them in my direction.

"Sorry", I manage to say, "Where do you want me to take these?" I point towards the tray with the three whiskey glasses.

"Miss Patty and the other two made that order, I think you'll find them by the fireplace. They left their table some time ago", he directs me.

Sure enough, I find them by the fireplace, all gathered in a circle, as if they needed to keep each other warm in spite of the temperature inside.

"Hey, ladies. I heard you ordered some whiskeys?" I hand them each a glass.

"Triona, darling, so good to see you," Miss Patty gives me a glance over. "How darling you look today! Burgundy is truly your color."

I don't let myself get distracted by the compliment, waiting for the other shoe to drop.

She surprises me, though, "We've had such a wonderful time here today! Do say thank you to your parents, dear. Your dad has outdone himself this year! That gravy was to die for!" The other two ladies smile and nod their heads along.

"I'll pass on the message! Now, if you'll excuse me…" and I take my leave unscathed. Maybe miracles do happen around the holidays.

I can't keep my eyes off of him. There's a sea of people separating us, but I keep dragging my eyes towards his table. He looks so nonchalant, and so happy talking to his parents. I catch him belly laugh a couple of times, and I wish I were braver to get closer to them and hear everything they are saying.

I feel for his parents, though. With his crazy schedule, I have no clue how often they get to see him. I couldn't even believe he had managed to get a few days off to be here this year. I could swear he had a game just after New Year's, so I wondered for how long he would be staying.

The time finally came where I could no longer avoid them, and I forced my feet to march in their direction. What should've taken me seconds, felt like minutes, but before I could decide against it, I'm in front of them.

"Heeee-y…"

"Triona!" Mrs. Noah cuts me off. She gets up and wraps me in the one of the best hugs in the world, "We haven't seen you in forever! How are you, sweetie? Your parents cannot give us enough updates!"

I could feel the blood rise up to my neck and cheeks, "Hi, Mrs. and Mr. Noah! I'm fine, thank you. How are you guys?"

I look around the table, sensing the awkwardness in waves. Knox is avoiding looking at me and is instead staring at the menu. Not that it had changed in the 15 years since the pub opened.

A couple of 'fines' sound across the table and I take advantage of the couple of dead seconds to not extend this interaction any longer, "Would you guys like to eat something or just drinks?"

"We wouldn't miss your dad's food for anything!" this one comes from Mr. Noah, who might've always been a man of few words, but was always excited at mealtime.

I smile at both of them, "Coming right up!"

I feel daggers hitting my back when I turn to leave, but I don't dare looking back. Because that had been a bit more draining than I expected and because I really wasn't looking forward to getting a do-over, I ask Nico to take care of their table, and walk into the kitchen to get some more space between us.

Between doing the dishes and helping my dad with platting, I barely notice the hour passing, and I'm scraping the last large pot when my mom enters the kitchen and announces that we should both come out and enjoy the end of the luncheon.

Everyone's happy and fed and even though some have already left, the pub is still packed with people chatting and drinking in circles and around tables.

I'm pouring myself a cider when I notice Mrs. Noah making her way towards the bar.

"Can I get you anything else to drink?" I ask her, trying to sound cheerful.

"Oh, no, sweetie, no more for me. I've already had a couple and if I drink anything else, I think I'll fall asleep right here," she laughs it off.

"I see what you mean…" I shrug my shoulders.

I try to keep myself busy, grabbing my cider and taking a sip, but I can sense that there's something she wants to say or ask me. It's the way she looks around us and in the direction of their table that allows me to read her easily.

"So, tell me about New Haven! How are things going for you up there?" she seems to force herself to ask.

I give her a rundown of things, from how lost I felt in the first year to landing next summer's internship. I don't go into detail because I don't want to bother her with things she might not be interested in, but I'm always happy to talk about what I've accomplished. Moving to another state all alone, though it is pretty common among undergraduates, was a little shocking to me. Whether because I was not living with my parents for the first time ever, or because of a relationship that I believed would be forever ending, the truth was harsh, and I struggled to acclimate to that new environment.

"So, I'm pretty thrilled to dip my feet in and see what it truly means to be an architect." I tell her.

"It all sounds great, Triona. I know how hard things can be when we're far away from the ones we love, so you should be very proud of yourself for everything you've done in these last few years," she smiles genuinely at me and squeezes my hand to prove it.

"Yeah…", I reflect on her words, being far away from the ones we love, and I wonder if she meant more than my parents. "What about you and Mr. Noah? How have you guys been with Knox around?" I don't know if the subject is too brittle to approach, but I can't help but wonder. "Do you get to visit him often?"

She looks at me and I notice a flash of sadness in her eyes, but her words sound like a true, proud mother, "Oh, we see him often enough. He's always inviting us to go watch him play, and you know his dad wouldn't miss an opportunity to coach him on the field," we both laugh at that. "And he's been in town a few times over the years, too. Whenever he has time off, he likes to surprise us with a visit or two." Her smile widens when she says, "And did you know he's taken us to Hawaii a couple of times too? It had always been my dream to go there, and he took us both on a trip right after he got drafted with the Bears."

I nod along, listening to how proud she speaks of her son, all the time thinking he had truly made it. He used to tell me all the time that once he had enough money, he would take his parents to Hawaii to thank them for everything they'd done for him over the years. He had also told me I'd be invited too, but we all know how that had turned out.

"That's truly incredible, Mrs. Noah, I'm certain he's so happy to have you with him and to be able to pay for your travels."

"Yes… I can see he loves it," her eyes scour the place once more, and I can sense her next topic before she opens her mouth again.

"You know, maybe it's not my place to say anything, but what kind of mother would I be if I didn't share my concerns from time to time? Knox struggled for a while at the beginning of his 2nd year in college. I didn't know if he would make it in Chicago all alone and with the pressure of it all. After the first few months, he seemed happy there, even though he wasn't first quarterback, you know? But they had told him he would be at the start of the school year, in August, so he really was focused on it, he was working hard. We thought everything was going okay, but after the summer, he just stopped calling us and wouldn't answer my messages neither", her eyes search mine, and I know what she's implying. "After a couple of weeks of radio silence, his dad bought a plane ticket and went there to see him. Make sure he was okay, you know?", she plays with her bracelet. "We knew he was still playing and was the team's main quarterback because we'd watch the college games on TV, but he was my little baby and I needed to know if he was okay outside the field too."

I can feel the back of my throat and my stomach is in a knot. Hearing these things about him makes me question whether I should have messaged him back then. That summer and the first semester in

New Haven was excruciating, I didn't feel like meeting new people, nor attending the parties thrown to welcome new students. I was barely living, hiding myself under textbooks and classes. I spent so much time asking for guidance in assignments and extra projects that my professors all knew me by name in the second month of school. All to keep me occupied, and not dwelling on a certain someone.

Mrs. Noah continued, "He didn't come home that Christmas. Did you know that?" she touched my hand and left hers wrapped around mine.

"No…", I breathe.

"Of course when he came home the summer after his one semester there, we figured it out. We understood he wasn't doing well, and he finally told us you guys had broken up. He never told us why…" she hid her face, probably ashamed of mentioning this to me. "You know… He never explained, Triona. His dad and I thought things would go back to normal at some point. You'd talk and clear everything out, maybe you could meet each other in New Haven, and everything would go back to normal. We believed that, you know?"

I nod my head, not trusting myself to speak right now. I move both hands and hold the bar counter to support my weight. I didn't expect this conversation today. On Christmas Eve… at the pub… with his mom. I want to go hide inside a cabinet and stay there until everyone leaves.

"I'm sorry, honey. I did not want to make you feel sad. I just wanted you to know that he did not have a nice time for a long time, just in case you thought any different," she sighs, "I know you're both doing great things now, and I can see how much Yale agrees with you."

I don't know what to tell her. Yes, I'm doing great most days. I learned to love college, and not just in the classroom. I met amazing people and I see them almost every day back there, I am very thankful for the opportunity I got to work alongside talented, successful architects next summer, and I don't even mind my love life.

Most days, I said. I also have terrible ones. And those hit me hard, and I can barely get up. But then, something happens. A text from a friend, a video that makes me laugh in the middle of the night, and sometimes, even just a long, hot shower, and I start seeing the light again. It could be months now that I haven't felt one of those lows.

"Well, I'm happy to see you're okay, honey. You look beautiful as ever, and I hope I can see your talented work soon." She comes around the bar and gives me a tight embrace. "I just thought you should know. Merry Christmas, honey." She squeezes my arms and goes back to her table.

12.

Finally, things start to die down after a few hours of intense labor, and a whole lot of food. I'm wiping down the counters when I see Liv and Sienna making their way towards his table. I feel a bit envious all of a sudden, and I hate it, so I focus my attention on replacing an empty keg in the draft machine. I can't imagine how many of these we've gone through today. Don't let our little town fool you, these people can drink.

"Hey, Tee, we're gonna leave now." I hear Sienna say above me.

I get up, swiping my hands over my legs. "Did you have fun?" I ask them both.

"Of course we had fun, Tee. But more importantly, I had great drinks," she winks at me.

I laugh at her, noticing she's a little tipsy, "Glad we could be of service."

"The food was delicious as always, Tee. We've already thanked your parents when we went over to say bye", Sienna points in their direction, surrounded by friends and neighbors. "We also wished a Merry Christmas to…" she whispers, "Ox", then louder, "Is that okay?"

I realize then that I never told them about us meeting after the bonfire. Everything had felt a little too raw to share, even with my two best friends, but I will have to tell them at some point. Maybe just not now with so many people around us.

"Of course it's okay, S", I look around us to make sure no one is interested in our conversation, "I need to tell you something later. Something happened."

Liv seems to sober up quickly at my words, "Whaaat?" she half-yells.

I pat her arm, "Don't yell! Shush!" I lean towards them and add, "I'll explain better another time, but we met."

They both gasp. These two, they truly are the best*est* of friends anyone could ask for.

"Untwist your panties, please. We met, and it went terribly," before they could ask any more questions that I didn't feel like answering yet, I continue, "No, we didn't fuck, Liv, and no, we didn't say we love each other, S. Now that your most urgent questions are out of the way, please give me tonight to spend time with my family, whom I haven't seen in too long, and then we can chat all about it and make up different scenarios as to why it went the way it did. Deal?"

They both nods their heads, "Can't believe you just said fuck and S didn't even flinch." Liv says looking at Sienna, who rolls her eyes back at Liv.

"We're leaving now, Tee. Do you need any help before we go?" Sienna asks me.

"No, we're all good. I think we'll be shutting down soon anyway, since mom will want to go home and take a nap before my aunts get here tonight."

We all hug, wish each other a Merry Christmas, and promise to meet after Christmas Day to talk about everything.

When they leave, I continue to get everything ready and clean at the bar. My parents won't open again until the 26th for lunch, but

I like to do as much as possible today, so they won't need to come in extra early that day.

As more and more people start to leave, I notice that Knox and his parents are also standing up and putting on their jackets. I look at my bag, hiding on a shelf under the counter, and I can feel its contents burning a hole through the fabric. I just told Sienna and Liv that I needed more time to process what happened to know what to tell them, but I know I will regret this moment if I at least don't try to speak to him. I know what he wanted to hear from our conversation, but I just couldn't let him in again. I don't think I would be able to survive another few months away from our hometown, if I'd have my heart broken again.

"Hey, do you have a minute?" I meet him halfway and smile at him, hoping that there's enough people near us that he won't feel comfortable neglecting me.

He puts his hands inside his jacket's pockets, and shrugs. "Sure." He turns to his parents and tells them he'll meet them at the house.

I signal towards the Christmas tree with my head, and tell him, "Let me just grab something, I'll be right back."

After rummaging through my bag and finding the wrapped gift, I make my way to the booth he's sitting on by the Christmas tree. I slide over, facing him. "This one's great." I look over at the ornaments on the tree and see a familiar one shaped as a compass. That makes me smile.

I can feel his eyes following mine and pausing at the different memories this place and this booth hold for us. Uncomfortable with his silence, I grab the little box and I push it across the table towards him. "I saw this the other day and thought you'd like it," I shrug, now feeling self-conscious of my gesture, "It's nothing special but it just made me think of you, and you know, Merry Christmas."

I hate how our last conversation ended, and how self-aware I am at the moment. We've always had an easy connection. He'd always make me feel comfortable and wouldn't let me overthink these moments. Now, he's making me squirm on purpose. His face remains stoic, his breathing even.

He takes it and lays it next to him, on the bench. "Thank you."

I exhale. "Knox, please don't be upset with me. You asked me a question and I answered. I really don't understand why you left so abruptly."

That makes him tick. "You don't know why?" His posture changes then. He's no longer saving his breath. "How could I not be upset that you went to Chicago a year after you broke up with me, a year after not answering any of my texts or calls!"

It feels like I've been slapped with his words. That knocked me out so hard that my back hits the seat.

"That's not fair, Knox. We broke up with each other. We both chose it", I take a deep breath before continuing, "And you're right. We had been broken up for almost a year. We weren't talking. And I'm not sure that I knew you were still in Chicago", I'm such a pretty little liar. "How was I supposed to know you'd even want to see me, Knox?"

His chest is moving so fast now, his breathing erratic. "Are you fucking joking right now? I tried so fucking hard! I wanted us to sort things out. I called you every fucking day for a month! Are you fucking with me?" He looks at me as if he truly wants an answer to his question. "Even if you didn't know I was in Chicago, you could have texted. You could have asked me!" He stops for a few seconds, probably waiting for me to step in and say something, but I just can't right now. "Triona, we spent years together. You saw me at my worst. Maybe we weren't together, dating anymore then, but you know I would have been happy to see you." He drops his head back and closes his eyes. "I thought we were supposed to be honest with each other." He enunciates, "Always."

He slides his legs to the side of the bench and stands up. Then, he leans over and grabs his gift. "Thanks for this." He shakes the gift in my direction. "Merry Christmas, Ina."

It's only a few minutes later that my body slowly wakes up. My ears are the first to awake, the loud voices bringing them back to the pub. My hands are next, touching the polished wood table, and I feel my feet too. I wiggle my toes inside my shoes, making sure they're also still alive. I inhale through my nose and count to five. I hold my breath for another five seconds, then exhale through my mouth, 1, 2, 3, 4... 5. Once I feel my breathing back to normal and my heart rate has slowed down, I push my feet against the floor and stand up.

Seeing my parents with only a few people left in the pub, I move towards them and tell my mom I'm tired and would like to go home. "Is that okay? Do you need an extra hand with anything?"

"No, darling, thank you. Go and rest a bit before tonight's feast! We'll meet you home soon. I need a little nap after being on my feet for so many hours."

I give her a tight hug and drop a kiss on my dad's cheek before grabbing my jacket and car keys.

I need a shower and to sleep this conversation off. I want to celebrate with my family tonight, and I can't keep thinking about him and his damned words. I just hope Santa will find me on the nice list and makes this Christmas a special one, because I sure need some magic right about now.

13.

I wake up to a dark room with wet hair sticking to my face. I feel around my nightstand to find my phone and when I light it up, it shows 6:11pm. I've slept for a little over an hour. I stretch my arms over my head and remove the cold hair from my face. My pillow is also wet and it's the most unpleasant feeling ever, so I throw it down on the floor. I lay there, hands on my stomach now, staring at the ceiling and I repeat some mantra words that I hope will keep me in check for the night. "I am happy. I am kind. I make my own decisions. I am calm. I am excited." I could throw in there a couple of motivational hairdressing techniques, but I'd like to get downstairs in time to help my mom and dad spruce things up a little and I'm sure my aunts and uncle will be arriving shortly.

Finally getting up, I connect my phone to the speakers in my bathroom and choose a Christmas playlist to get in the holiday spirit. I decide against curling my hair, so I just dry it and spend a few more minutes on my makeup. Red and green glitter across my eyelids and a nude lip to balance it out. I like my mascara clumpy and in-your-face, so I apply a few layers before I'm happy with the result. A spritz of perfume behind my ears, my wrists and on top of my hair for good measure, and I'm ready. I look down and forgot I was still in my pajamas, but a good, stretchy pair of leggings and an ugly Christmas sweater are the formal attire in my family, so I quickly throw those on, and I'm jumping off the last stair when I hear my parents singing in the kitchen.

Peeking through the door, I see them dancing to an old Christmas ballad while my dad sings and my mom mostly giggles. The love they still have for each other surprises me every time I experience it. It's so wonderful to see them enjoy life together. This is what I want one day. They may bicker and sass at each other from time to time, but when the world quietens, they always find each other and love each other with such honesty that it would frighten most. It's these moments that I cherish, and some might say that growing up around such a love could impact how you see your own relationships. How fearful you might feel if things seem a little challenging, or how easy it is to question yourself and the love you *think* you feel. Is it real? When the lights go out, will you still be there for me? When we fight, will I still have your love and concern? Or will you shut me down? The kind of love that transpires between my parents is like in the movies. And how could you ever live up to that?

"Mo stór, there you are!" my dad interrupts my reverie, "Did you get some rest?" He comes over and hugs me.

"I slept like the dead. What about you guys? Did you manage to get any rest? When did you get back?"

"We left not long after you, and I closed my eyes for a half hour. Your dad was snoring beside me, though, so he feels very energetic as you can see."

My dad feigns disbelief. "Me? Snoring? How could that be, my love? This is the first time I'm hearing this." He looks pensive for a second and says, "Are you sure you weren't dreaming?"

My mom rolls her eyes at him and I laugh. "He's not wrong, mom. You mention his snoring every time you can. I think the whole town knows about it."

Before any of us can answer, the bell rings, followed by a voice a few seconds later, "Where's my favorite niece?"

Dad's youngest sister has never hidden her love for me. I was the first baby in the family and she used to spoil me rotten whenever she came to visit. "Hey, aunt Melinda!" She wraps her arms around me, and I can immediately smell her signature perfume. "I missed you!", I add.

"Let me look at you, now." She steps back and makes me twirl like I'm 5. "Good golly, look at those perfect round hips. When did you become so incredibly curvy? You're stealing the show!" Aunt Melinda always loved to shower me with compliments, even if they sounded just as weird as they could get.

"I guess growing up does this to you", I shrug my shoulders. "And Yale has really, really great food."

"Good for you, hon!" She moves around me and greets my parents while I welcome my other aunt, dad's oldest sister, her husband and my two younger cousins.

Once we've done the usual greetings and catch up, we all move to the dining room to start off our meal. Mom stands up and clinks her glass.

"I don't want to steal my husband's spotlight, as he's usually the one for speeches, but I couldn't let this opportunity escape me. My most precious, loving daughter is home." She tears up. "We all missed you like crazy, and God knows your dad has been nagging me for years just to fill up the void you've left in our home." Everyone laughs at that. "But now you're here, even if for only a short while… you're home. This will forever be your home, and honey, you can come back whenever you want."

Now I feel like tearing up as well. Looking around the table, seeing my aunts and uncle, my cousins and my parents, all in one room, finally, I feel the heavy weight of what I've been missing for far too long.

"I don't want to make this any longer, but we're so happy you're here, Triona. We wouldn't want it any other way. Merry Christmas, everybody, cheers!"

We all cheer and clink our glasses filled with our traditional punch with Irish hot whiskey. I let the liquid burn down my throat, not used to how strong it feels anymore.

"Who wants some mince pies?" auntie Melinda asks.

Everyone shoots their hand in the air. Hers are the best mince pies I've ever had. We fill our bellies with roast turkey and potatoes, the same meal we had at the pub earlier today, and none of us minds repeating it because it's *that* good. If you'd look around the table, you'd see a family who loves each other and always has fun spending time together. When I was younger, we used to spend time with the entire family, my mom's brother included. Then, everyone started getting married and having babies, and even though they don't live too far from our town, they spend the holidays with their in-laws. I grew up with two cousins, who are closer in age to me, and we'd love running around the house pretending to be superheroes, hiding under the bed or in the closet to catch bad guys. Brennan, who's only a year younger than me, and Leigh, who's the baby cousin in my mom's side of the family - though she's only 4 years younger than Brennan - used to come over often, not just for the holidays. I miss them, too. I have to text them, see if they'd like to meet soon.

We're all digging into the desserts now, some staples on the table. The sherry trifle is my uncle's territory, and he's always proud and makes it a ceremony to serve people. He's not wrong, it's a pretty good sherry trifle.

"So, Triona, how are you doing at Yale? Lauren is starting to think of colleges, and I'm sure she'd love to hear about your experience", my aunt Maeve says about her daughter.

"Oh, I'm loving it there, aunt Maeve. The campus is beautiful, and most people are quite helpful. When I first arrived, I'd get lost pretty regularly, but I would just ask people where I was supposed to go, and I'd get there eventually. If you wanna visit one day, Lauren, you're more than welcome to come." She smiles eagerly at me; I got her to get off her phone for a few seconds.

"She'd love that, honey. Thank you for suggesting it!" aunt Maeve says to me. "And what about any dates? Are you seeing anyone?"

I can feel the whole table staring at me now, forks midair, not a swallow happening, everyone waiting for my answer. "No… No one to write home about, auntie."

The clatter of silverware against plates restarts, and everyone pretends to be busy.

"She'll find someone when she feels like it," aunt Melinda comes to my rescue, "Look at me, I'm 42 and I'm still dating!" She winks at me.

My dad intervenes then, "She can focus on school for now, and maybe once she's started her career, she can think of dating."

"Are you living in the 40s, brother of mine? A woman has to be one-dimensional now?" Aunt Melinda loves to pick on my dad. She always pretends to be much more open-minded because of their age difference. This annoys my dad every time. There's only a 5 years' gap between them.

"Melinda, I'm saying she should work. I don't think that's a very 40s belief. And she can do whatever she wants, but I've always told her she's the first one to go to college. She should be proud of herself and let that thought motivate her."

"She cannot carry around that pressure, Mikey. It's not her job to be the first one in the family to achieve more. I can't believe you put her under that much pressure. That's not how mom raised us."

"Guys, stop, please. We're all happy, remember? It's okay, aunt Melinda. I'm fine." I try to appease them.

"No, it's not okay, honey. We're all so proud of you", she pauses and holds my hands in hers, "You've accomplished what none of us ever have, that's true, but that doesn't mean you have to put your life on hold and only see that degree as your only reason of achievement, you're so much more than your studies and your talent."

"Of course she is! I've never said otherwise. She's incredibly talented, and beautiful, and kind-hearted, and funny! And she loves so deeply that we," he looks at my mom, "we feel her love all the way from Connecticut."

"Oh my goodness, I didn't know this would turn into a compliment fest. If I'd known, I'd have dressed up in my most fabulous dress, guys!" I feign excitement.

"The truth is, we all know that she could and *should* be dating if she wants to. Find a pretty bum and chase it", aunt Melinda likes to sound crass but with elegance, unlike Liv. "Now, are you happy to be back, dear?"

It sounds like their little feud is over for now. "Yes, of course, I am. I get to see you all." I smile around the table. "And I got to spend time with Liv and Sienna, too, so I'd say this was a very successful trip."

When everyone's distracted eating their trifle and Christmas pudding, aunt Melinda leans into my chair and whispers, "Have you seen him? Your parents told me he's in town."

Oh, my family has a way of getting intertwined in everyone's business, and I adore them to death, but it's been 4 years that, between calls and messages, everyone always gets to ask about Knox. I want to yell that I don't care, I don't know, and I don't wanna hear his name again. But it's my aunt Melinda asking, and I know she doesn't have any ill intentions, she's only asking because she worries about me. And I try to keep that thought in mind when I answer her. "He's in town. And we've met, but I really would love to not think about him tonight, aunt Melinda."

She must see the hurt and pleading in my eyes because she only adds, "You know, sometimes, letting it out helps the hurt lift from your heart." She gives me a quick kiss and we go back to eating dessert.

After a few rounds of board games, a tradition we have in our family, we're tired and it's almost midnight, so we start opening gifts earlier than usual. Everyone loves seeing what others get, and we all cheer each other, which makes this moment extra special. My parents offer me beautiful jewelry and a box of different jams that I can take with me and keep in the mini-fridge I have in my dorm room.

It's past 1am when we're in the entryway, hugging and wishing each other a good night. We'll all meet here again tomorrow to celebrate Christmas Day like we do every year, but we still hug like we won't see each other again for another year.

I'm in my bedroom getting into my pajamas and aunt Melinda's words keep running in my mind. Letting things out might help the hurt I've been storing away for too long. Maybe being honest with myself first will lift this weight on my heart I've been feeling for many years. But what is the truth exactly? What do I need to let out to help me?

I lay on my stomach, hands supporting my chin, and I close my eyes. I go over our past. The happy memories, 'I was happy', I say out loud. Is that it? Do I need to admit that I was the happiest I've ever felt? I don't think I've ever hidden that from myself. It's hard to say it out loud because I fear I may never be that happy again, but I know in my heart that our time together made me the happiest. I sit up against my bed frame now and focus on what I've been hiding instead. Maybe not only from myself.

Something immediately comes to my mind and tears pool in my eyes. I know what I need to let out. Even if there's more to this, I remember something that I lied about and maybe, just maybe, I can dissipate some of this sadness that I've been stuck in. But will it truly help? That makes me nervous.

I grab my phone, open my texts and click on 'new message'. Finding his contact, I type "Honesty check. I did go to Chicago for you" and press send.

I fall asleep holding onto my phone, waiting for an answer that never came.

14.

A couple of days later, I'm out shopping with Liv and Sienna in Providence, and we've been updating each other on our Christmases.

"I still can't believe your nanny gave you a book on how to date like a lady in the 21st century," I laugh, looking at Liv.

"Tell me about it! I spent an hour lecturing my whole family on the problematic subject. I mean, it's not even like I don't know how to date. But to imply I'm not a lady..." she pauses, "I mean, c'mon!" And she strikes a pose, pushing her boobs out and pouting her mouth while batting her eyelashes. "Who would look at me and not immediately think of the word 'lady'?

We all laugh looking at her. "You're perfect the way you are, Olive", Sienna moves towards her. "And I think any person should be allowed to date however they see fit. I mean, you've explored a lot. A l-o-t" she enunciates. "And I think that's exactly what we should be doing. How are you supposed to know yourself if you haven't met all sorts of people? Or even dated all sorts of people?" She shrugs.

Liv and I are staring at her, dumbfounded. Who's this new Sienna and what does she mean with we should all be exploring. I didn't know she had that word in her dictionary.

"What the fuck are you talking about?" Liv screams in her face. "I know you haven't just said you think you should be exploring people." She looks at me trying to find a sign this is all a big joke we're playing on her. I shrug, my face saying, 'I don't know what's happening either.' Liv stares back at Sienna, "*Who* have you been exploring, Sienna?"

"Oh my God, Liv, you're so dramatic." She dismisses her with a brush of her hand and moves over to a rack full of vintage Levi's. "I'm just saying we're in our early 20s and I'm all for exploring my options."

I don't know what to say. Clearly, Liv doesn't know what to say either. We're both glued to our spot, arms carrying one too many clothes, and we have nothing to say. I don't think I've ever seen Liv this speechless.

"Guys, stop it now." Sienna tells us. "You always act like I'm such a prude." She pouts and puffs out her chest, "Well, I'm not."

"I may not have a long list of people, but I know things..." and she tries to say confidently, "I've fucked, you know..." But the blush creeping up her neck tells us she doesn't really love using that word.

"S, c'mon. You don't have to explain yourself to us. And we know you're not a prude. We're just playing with you." I add, "And please, don't use the word fuck again if you don't feel like it. It's not a badge of promiscuity. Right, Liv?" I nudge her.

She dissolves into being her cool self, "Of course not, S! I also make love from time to time." She bats her eyelashes at her. "And just let me know if you need any ideas of how to explore some more." She jumps up and down in the middle of the thrift store.

"Deal." Sienna agrees.

Spending too many hours stepping into stores and being greeted by the cold air outside isn't always my idea of fun but being with Liv and Sienna makes up for it. This shopping area in Providence is incredibly well adorned with Christmas lights and feels very festive. There are trucks serving yummy food and hot drinks to the few people who venture the cold and don't mind staying outside in this season. My cheeks feel like they're constantly frozen and never truly warm up, even though we spent a lot of time browsing through the different stores. So, after shopping for too long and spending too much money, us three sit at a coffee shop to rest our feet and consume well-needed doughnuts and hot chocolate, extra whipped cream for me.

"So, Tee, we haven't forgotten about what you promised us at the luncheon." Sienna starts.

"Yeah, Tee, what's happened with you two?"

"Well, after I left the Swing, I went home and was so pissed off at him. Do you remember how he didn't even say anything to me, S?" I look at Liv and explain, "He came over when we were all in a group just chatting and he pretended I didn't even exist. It was just too much to bear. It had been the second time he did that in just a short amount of time, so I couldn't stay any longer, you know…"

I'm met with sympathy looks and nods from both of them.

"Anyway, I was back home and fell asleep going over everything. And you won't guess what happened later."

"What?" Sienna's eyes bulging from her face, anticipating my next words.

"I woke up to a clicking sound." Their faces seem confused for a few seconds until realization crosses them both at the same time. "Yep. It was Knox at my window," I add in a sigh, "Like he used to."

"Oh-my-god!"

"Holy fuck, Tee!"

I nod at them, agreeing with their reactions. "Trust me, I know. I couldn't believe it myself." After a couple of seconds, I carry on, "I was so puzzled at first, I didn't even know if I was sleeping or not. I truly thought it had been my constant thinking of him since coming home that had made me imagine the sound."

"I bet…" Sienna whispers.

"So, I opened the window, he climbed up, and we were just there. Back in my bedroom, just like we were in high school again." I let my body go through the emotions of remembering what had happened that night. The sudden fear flowing into understanding and then, the jitters that assaulted me seeing him climb up the roof. I fall back into my chair, looking at my two best friends, and can see how worried they feel for me.

"I really didn't expect him there, especially not after him having the opportunity to speak to me and plainly just refusing. So, my thoughts exactly were, why is this happening now. And here." I bend over the table and gesture with my hands, "In my effing bedroom where every inch reminds me of him. As if I needed the extra memories, you know."

A couple of 'yeahs' echo between us and Liv asks, "Okay, but what did he say? And what were you wearing?"

That makes me laugh and roll my eyes at the same time. "I was in my pajamas, Liv, what else? I was sleeping! I didn't have time to think about 'Oh, I should definitely change for Knox, whom I haven't spoken to in forever, and don't even know why he's here'. I'll definitely keep that in mind for next time, Liv."

"Next time?" Sienna murmurs.

"Just an expression, S. Look, guys, it was bad, okay? It started out okay, I guess. I called him Oxie." I get understanding nods. "He called me Ina as well. We talked about school, his career, just life in general. It was awkward at first, but we fell into a comfortable conversation for a while."

"And…?"

"And then, he said something about how I'm not in his life anymore, so I can't talk about what I don't know. I left him up in my room and went to the kitchen then. I needed some distance between us in that moment. I needed to feel like I could breathe and think things through. I thought he would leave, though. But he came down and met me in the kitchen." I pause to sip my hot chocolate and think about my next words. "Do you know how when you truly know someone, you move alongside each other like you're dancing a waltz?

Your movements fluid, mirrored almost. It felt like that. It was scary how normal it felt, somehow.”

“I get that,” Sienna sighs.

Liv and I look at her, wondering why she said in that way.

“He asked me a tough question. I denied it. He got upset. Like I had broken his heart type of upset. And he left.”

I straighten my back against the chair. “That’s it. It went terribly. And I felt so empty afterwards, it reminded me of how numb I was 4 years ago. I do not want to feel that way, ever again, guys. I don’t think I could survive it this time.”

My words leave my lips, but my body swallows each and every one of them, experiencing them as if they were already real. Allowing my mind to travel to these places is never a good idea for me. It can affect my mood for the entire day if I let it. I start thinking about the ‘what ifs’, an imaginary future that seems bleak. I try to focus on the other side of things. My career, my love for designing, my parents. I allow my mind to think about these happy things, dwell on them even, because they bring me peace.

“Tee, why did he get upset? What did he ask you?” Liv asks me.

I take a deep breath. I knew they were going to ask me about this specifically. They would, obviously. It’s still hard to admit, though, because I didn’t tell them back then when I went to Chicago. And even though I have already admitted it to him, it still feels heavy to say it out loud.

“I went to Chicago for a weekend about a year after we broke up.” They gasp at my words. “Yeah… I told him about it, unintentionally, and he asked me if I had gone there for him.” I pause, thinking about the truth. “I lied to him.”

“You told him no”, Sienna adds.

“Yes. I told him it hadn’t been for him… which was a lie.” I admit, more to myself than to them.

“Oh-my… Why didn’t you tell us about it back then?” Liv asks, shocked.

I shrug, "I don't know… I guess I didn't know why I was going there in the first place. It's not like I had a plan. I booked a flight without thinking about it. I just did it."

"That doesn't sound like you, at all." Sienna's concerned look warms my heart.

"I know, it wasn't like me. I booked a flight and when I was on the plane, I truly thought, 'what am I doing? Maybe I should go back' and I thought staying at the airport would be a great idea. I truly thought that I could spend the night at the airport and wait for my flight back."

"That sounds like a terrible plan." Liv rolls her eyes.

I laugh, "Yeah, it was, but I got so scared all of a sudden. I was afraid of running into him, and my reasoning was that staying at the airport would prevent that from happening."

Carrying on, I tell them, "I didn't, anyway. I went to my hotel, and I even explored the city a bit. I forced myself to go out and convinced myself that it was a school trip. I had worked hard and I deserved a weekend off. It just so happened to be in his new city." I shrug and whisper, "I went to his college too."

Liv and Sienna both gasp and yell, "What! You were there, truly there?"

"Yep. I didn't want to text him, but I thought, if I see him, then that's my sign. If I don't, I have to move on."

"Now, that sounds like the stupidest thing I've ever heard!" Liv never shies away from saying what she truly believes.

"I know you guys don't really believe in these things, but what can I say, I do. And it just seemed the right thing to do at the time. I'm not saying it was smart or the best plan, but it's what happened. Anyway, obviously, I didn't see him, and I left the next morning. I couldn't bring myself to admit all this to him that night, though. And it wouldn't have changed any outcome, so I thought it was best for me to keep that tiny shred of pride I still had."

They share a look among themselves that makes me question what they're thinking about.

"What? What did you just do?" I point at them, moving my finger from Sienna to Liv.

They exchange another look before Sienna speaks up, "Look, we didn't say anything because you were at the lowest we'd ever seen you, Tee. We didn't want to disturb things, and you closed up on us. We couldn't reach you for a while, and you know it. You stopped sharing and we just didn't know what would be best at the time."

"What are you talking about? What didn't you tell me?"

Sienna looks scared, and Liv steps in, "Tee, Knox came back to town at the end of summer. He texted and asked to meet us both. I was still in town, so we met him."

"Wha-?"

She puts her hand over mine and adds, "We met at the corner café, and he was a mess, Tee. He looked so heartbroken, and he just wanted to know if we'd had any contact with you at all because you weren't answering his messages."

I don't know what to feel right now. I can't say I don't understand their thought process, I was a mess too, I went to New Haven right after high school ended and I stopped talking to them every day. But I still wish they had told me they met him.

"He begged us to give him anything. Any information we had on you. If you were okay, and if you had started school", Sienna adds.

"Yeah." Liv looks at Sienna again, and I can see an approval from both of them. "There's more, Tee. This is why we decided to not tell you back then. We truly thought it wouldn't matter; we thought you were too hurt to want to hear this."

Sienna is staring at her hands now and I can tell this has been weighing on them. Liv seems to struggle for words. They're tag-teaming this conversation.

"He told us he wished you could be in the same city. He regretted not waiting to hear from Cornell or Columbia before accepting U of Chicago so promptly. He said he knew you'd get into Yale, and he wished you guys could have been near each other." Sienna does her best to tell me this story.

"We could tell he wanted to be with you. He wanted to experience college with you. And he looked so remorseful that he hadn't waited to hear from other schools that were closer to Yale", Liv finishes.

I'm struggling for words now. I'm aware that we both agreed we couldn't continue dating with so many miles between us. And when I got my letter of acceptance to Yale, that had been the end point. We would be even further away, and I couldn't afford to visit both him and my parents, so we would've ended up only seeing each other around the holidays and summer. The only logical step we both agreed on was to break up. It had happened one evening on the phone. I told him my news, excited to have gotten into one of the most privileged colleges in the country, and he had been so thrilled for me too. I thought our conversation would stay around that topic. That I would dream about the different classes I would attend, and how exciting it would all feel for the first time. I thought we wouldn't veer into dangerous territory, but that's exactly what happened. He told me he wouldn't have time to go visit me between classes and practice, and that he needed to focus even more on showing his coaches how much he wanted to be there. He was hoping for the quarterback's position in the new season, and he was very clear that he needed to step up. And that had been the beginning of the end. We argued for the next two hours, spewing things that had no place in a loving relationship, and we both felt defeated by the end of it all. I had let out the words 'Maybe we just need to break up and this way no one will need to visit anyone else.' And he answered, 'You're right.' That had been it. Two plus years of struggles, love and our whole fucking lives intertwined, just disappeared. We had hung up the phone and never spoken again.

Trust me, I wanted to. I really wanted to call him and take it all back. I wanted to beg him to keep trying. I wanted to promise him I would go anywhere he needed me to. That I would be the one traveling to see him every other month. I wanted to turn back time every second of every day for three weeks. After that hurt and pain, came anger. I was livid at him for leaving me that way. So I erased everything that reminded me of him from my bedroom. I deleted all our text messages. I blocked his number – though it didn't last after the summer - and deleted him from my social media. I had only kept a few things of his, and they were all stashed in a box on the top shelf of my closet, hidden behind a forgotten pair of roller skates and my painting supplies. Hobbies that were also left in the past.

"I get it," I sigh, "I don't know what would have happened either. I'm not entirely sure that I'd have wanted to know back then."

"We only did it because we thought it was the best for you, Tee. Please, believe that." Sienna begged.

"I know, guys." Looking at their concerned faces, I add, "Truly." I close my eyes and ponder my next words. "The truth is that I still felt so hurt by him back then. I blamed him for not trying harder, for not fighting for us. But I also think there was a part of me that didn't believe we were worth saving. My parents have the best kind of love I've ever seen. Maybe not everyone would say so, but to me, and to my limited experience, they're what I have as a standard, you know? And Knox and I went through so many hardships. We had been dating for only a few months when he got injured, damn. We went from cute dates at the Swing, hoping for a stolen kiss, to a full-blown adult relationship with me taking care of him and dividing my life between school and him." I look at them, searching for understanding in their faces. When I find it, I carry on, "I'm not saying I want to take it back, I loved us. I loved *him*. But I also felt the pressure of going to college, focusing on that and becoming an architect. And he, well, he had an amazing future ahead of him too. In a way, I guess, I didn't want to slow him down. Does that make sense?"

Liv whispers, "Yeah…"

Sienna adds, "I guess so. But Tee, a relationship isn't supposed to be easy. Love is. The love you have for one another is easy. Should be easy, anyway. But a relationship, that's hard work. Your love for each other sometimes blinds you to things you wouldn't accept from anyone else, or you get so used to your relationship that you forget to nurture it too. So, love is easy, but relationships definitely aren't."

Liv and I, for what seems the millionth time, are staring at Sienna, wondering what's been happening in her life that she's chosen not to share with us yet.

"Your parents are amazing, Tee. No question about that. But I'm sure if you'd ask them, they would also tell you that their relationship hasn't been easy. How could it be? Life isn't easy, and it throws things at you that you could never expect. I don't believe love is everything, and it is not enough to make a relationship work, but how would you know if you both quit before even trying?"

Her words mess with my heart more than I was prepared. I had been scared. I was 18 and scared of the big, bright future I was supposed to have. And all of a sudden, he wasn't a part of it. And that had been easier to accept than the fact that we could try and fail. What would have happened then? I would have been even more heartbroken.

"I don't know what to say, S… You're right. Of course, you're right. But 18-year-old Tee didn't have 22-year-old-wise you, so I made my decision then. Maybe it wasn't the best one, but it felt like the one I needed to make back then. Do I regret it? Almost every day. But I can't focus on something that I have no control over now. I can't let myself be stuck in the past and hope for a miracle. He moved on long ago, and I've accepted it. He has such a successful future ahead of him now, there's nothing I can do about it."

And wasn't that the truth? Knox had also made a decision, and I just couldn't keep thinking about the past. I felt like putting some distance between myself and my town. Everything felt more real and heavier here.

"Let's go, I wanna go home and take a bath. I feel like I'm gonna be sore from all this shopping", I tell them.

We make our way back to the car, and Liv drops me off at home first. During the drive, all I could think about was how he had come back for me, in a way.

15.

It was a scorching summer day, a couple of weeks before his surgery, and he told me to get ready and that he would pick me up at home. I didn't know where we were going, but he asked me to wear something comfortable.

I keep staring out the window, hoping to catch a glimpse of his Ford pickup. My heart is racing, and I feel like this is our first date. After making a hole through my bedroom floor from how much I've been walking around in circles, I hear an engine and run to the window again. Hiding behind the curtains so he cannot see me, I feel my heart drop the moment he opens his door and steps out. The easy smile he always has on his lips greets me first, then I look at him. He's wearing a fitted t-shirt that hugs his biceps in my favorite way, and the brown shorts that I love staring at from the back. In this moment, looking at him without having his eyes on me yet, I am assaulted by my love for him. In the shortest amount of time, I have let him reach inside me and open my heart fully to him. His silly jokes and his serious way of considering the world, the care he has for me and his closest friends, and the way he's so extroverted that it pains me, but I still love that about him. He's made me want to step outside and see the world through his eyes. He allowed me to be carefree, even if only in small intakes.

He looks up and smiles. I bet he knows I'm staring at him even though he cannot see me. I shake my head and laugh. He sees through me sometimes.

I meet him outside and he lets his eyes drag from my head to my toes. "Hey, what you looking at?" I tease him.

"Just appreciating the fact you listened to me when I said you should be comfy."

"Of course I paid attention." I look down at my clothes. "Is this not okay?"

"Yeah, it's okay, but I might get a little distracted." He gives me another glance over.

I roll my eyes at him. He's in a fun mood today, after the last months of so many ups and downs concerning his recovery and soon surgery, I'm happy to see him feel this light. "As if you didn't wear those exact shorts on purpose because I told you…" I whisper, "what I think about them."

He pulls me into him, "I wore them just for you, Ina." And he wraps me up in his arms, hugging me for a couple of minutes before kissing me softly on the lips.

I had never been hugged before he did it for the first time. Well, I had been obviously hugged, but not in the way he did it. It surprised me so much that one day he just greeted me that way one day that it took me several seconds to relax into him. His arms snaked around my back and he pushed me flat against his body. He didn't let go after a couple of seconds like a normal person, though. No, he hugged me properly for a full minute before letting go. I think that had been one of the moments where my heart cracked a little, and I knew then that he would forever change my life.

"Hi, you." He breathes in my mouth. "I missed you."

I giggle, "You saw me yesterday."

"I missed you anyway." He kisses my forehead.

"Ready to go?" He pulls away, a smile plastered on his face.

I nod ecstatically, worried my mouth wouldn't let any words out properly right now. I feel weak in the knees, and I'm not the one in need of a surgery.

We drive for a few minutes in silence. I love stealing glances at his profile when he drives. Not willing to let it get the best of me, I interrupt the tension I'm starting to feel and ask him, "Where are we going?"

"Some things are worth the wait, Ina." He smiles in my direction, eyes off the road for a second.

"I guess so… Let's play a game then. Would you rather?"

"Sure. You go first?"

I think about my question for a minute or so, trying to come up with something we haven't discussed yet. "I know! Would you rather swim in a pool of Nutella or in a pool of maple syrup?"

His laughter immediately fills the space around us. When he finally stops laughing, he answers, "I'm gonna go with the pool of maple syrup. How would you even swim in Nutella? You wouldn't be able to move!"

"Hmmm… I guess you're right. But you could eat your way out! Maple syrup's delicious, but I wouldn't be able to eat my way out of it." I make a face that resembles the green, nauseous emoji.

"Right. I thought the question was about swimming in it, though." He laughs at me again.

I roll my eyes at him. "Yeah, but you can do whatever you want in the pool."

"Okay, okay, I'll still choose maple syrup."

"Yummy choice either way. Now it's your turn!"

He doesn't hesitate for a second, the question at the tip of his tongue, "Would you rather be one of the world's leading experts in a single field or be the most well-rounded and versatile person in the world?"

These two questions summed up our relationship pretty darn well. Here I was, talking about spreads, and he was asking me a more serious question. People look at him and would never guess he is surrounded by these life questions, always thinking about the next thing to ponder on. It's easy to get lost in his good looks, and I can't deny that contributed to my liking of him at first, but it's been his heart, mind and soul that I've fallen completely in love with.

"Oxie, you truly ask such complex questions first thing off in the morning. I wish I knew everything there is to know about architecture, I'll tell you that. But I also feel intrigued by how things change, so if I were the leading expert of architecture, does that mean I wouldn't have anything else to learn?" I speak more to myself than him, but he gives me his opinion nonetheless.

"I don't think being an expert means you've learned everything you have to. But the continuous learning is what makes an expert, in my opinion."

"Yeah, I guess that makes sense. So I guess I'd love to have that sort of badge, you know. Be the person people would come to to ask for advice."

"That makes sense, Ina. I think most people strive for a sense of accomplishment and that's easily measured by how others perceive you. It's sad to think that we need other people to prove how good we are at something, but I guess that's just what we're taught."

"That sounds a bit dreary, but I think you're right. I think it also comes from the fact that we're taught older people are wiser, so we look up to them and think of them as role models. So, when you gain experience in whatever it is, you'll feel like others should look up to you and want your guidance. It comes with age. Not that it's a good measure for everyone, but I get it."

We spend the next quarter of an hour discussing our 7-year plan. Where we see ourselves and what we would like to accomplish. It's so easy to envision life alongside him. Not only with him in my life, but he truly makes me comfortable enough to share my craziest dreams. I could tell him literally anything and all he would do was nod and ask me a follow-up question, or say, 'I see that for you.'

In these seemingly insignificant moments, our relationship grew more and more. I couldn't bear the thought of doing life without him in it anymore. The new school year would feel so weird without him there, in the hallways, waiting for me outside my classroom. Eating lunch together and picking him up at home every day for a couple of months after his injury.

"Ready?" He looks at me, eagerly.

He makes a turn and I immediately recognize the sign for the indoor climbing place two towns over.

"Oh-my-god! Are we going climbing?" I feel like jumping inside the truck. "But what about your knee? Can you climb?"

"Well, not really, but I thought I could be your belayer while you climb. And we can get iced teas and pancakes across the street after. Whatcha think?"

I unbuckle my seatbelt and jump towards him, hugging him tightly. "It's the best idea ever!"

Just like this memory, there are a million others that make up the puzzle that was our relationship. Being back in our hometown not only reminds me of him, but every part of it *is* him. In my mind, every corner and traffic light belonged to him. I didn't come back for long because the mere thought of being invaded by images of him, of us around town consumed me to the point that I couldn't breathe. Only over a year after we broke up did I feel confident enough to think about him without bawling my eyes out in under two seconds. And still, it took a lot of strength to not let myself drown in feelings of guilt and shame over how things ended.

But here I was now, back in our hometown, for Christmas, of all times, and the flashbacks still invaded me every day. I don't think I could handle it for much longer… I felt safer when there was a lot more space between us. With my new routine and people who had never met him, never even talked about him, not as my ex, anyway. I had an urging feeling that I needed to go away.

I open the 'three musketeers' chat and type, "I think I'm gonna go back early."

Liv answers the next second with a GIF of a cat with his tongue slightly hanging out and a stunned look on its face, and it reads 'whaaaaaaaaaaaat'.

Sienna also replies right after, 'Back to New Haven? Why?? When??'

I sigh, knowing fully well these were the reactions they would have. I don't blame them, I also surprised myself. 'I don't feel like I can do this anymore. I tried, and I did it well for a few days. Now, it's time for me to go.'

Before any of them replies, I add, 'Anyway, got an email early this morning and a professor gave me the green light on a project for extra credit, so I'm gonna work on that before the New Year.'

'No way!' Liv texts back.

'Yeah, you can't just leave, Tee. When are you thinking about going?', Sienna adds to the chat.

'Don't know. Maybe the day after tomorrow. I'll tell my parents tonight and I can help out at the pub tonight, so they don't think I'm just bailing on them.'

Liv sends us another GIF, this time of a cat dancing with sunglasses on. She seems to come up with the only logical response to my leaving.

I send them a laughing GIF, 'Sure. Let's go out! I'll party with you guys and we can pretend it's New Year's.'

'Providence then? To the club S seems so keen on going to?', Liv teases Sienna. I can hear her tone through the phone.

'Deal!'

That decides it. We're going out before I leave, and I'm going back sooner than planned. Who didn't see this coming, anyway? I sure did… I guess lying to yourself has a way of catching up to you sooner or later, but I'm running off again, so hopefully it won't catch me before I'm far away.

16.

The music is loud, I feel my body pumping to the rhythm of the bass, and I already feel sticky, even though we haven't been here for long. For whatever reason, we didn't have to wait outside, but the queue was as long as I remember this place always having. It's one of the only few clubs in a 20 miles radius, so people from the surrounding towns all come here when they want to go dancing. Sienna led us straight to the bodyguards and they just let us in. Liv and I had exchanged quizzical looks but didn't say anything to her.

Sienna grabbed us all drinks and we were now making our way towards a private booth in the back, above the dance floor. Again, Liv and I don't quite get what's happening, but we're either too happy or a little tipsy to think this through right now.

"Best seats in the house!" Sienna shouts in our direction, "This way we don't have to worry about our coats and bags. We can keep them all here, and Sam will keep an eye on our things when we go dancing." She points towards another bodyguard, who's near the bottom of the stairs.

With the music booming in our ears and the lights shadowing our faces, Sienna doesn't seem to notice my inquiring face. That, or she doesn't want to acknowledge it.

"Guys, I can't believe we're right here!" Liv grabs our hands, one on each side of her, and jumps up and down. "S, how many times did you refuse to come out with us back in high school? And look at you now, all VIP and shit."

We all laugh and hug each other, bubbling energy running through us. All I want is to go onto the dance floor and forget about anything else that is happening in my life right now. I look at them both and gesture, 'Dance?', pointing towards the crowd. They nod, and we're going down the stairs, shuffling through bodies, wanting to be near the DJ table. We spend the next few songs dancing away, showing off our new moves to each other, laughing and partying like we're 18 again. I can feel the sweat pooling at the back of my neck, so I lift my hair and fan myself with my hand, trying to keep cool. "S, do you happen to have a magic restroom in here?" We all know that going to the restroom at the club isn't the best experience, it always takes forever and the things you see could never be erased from your memory.

She shouts back at me, "Yes! Go there," she points to the opposite direction of where we are, behind all the bodies around us, "Red door. Ask for Neil, say you're with me."

What the heck, I look at her and she's as serious as she can be. I shrug, for what seems the millionth time, not wanting to deal with whatever's happening tonight. I move across the floor, avoiding clashing into bodies, and soon I see the red door Sienna mentioned. I say her name and I'm told to go to the first door on the right. Sure enough, it's a restroom, and when I close the door, I can hear the whole club quieten down, my ears happy to have a couple of minutes of toned-down club music.

I splash my face and neck, trying to cool down. Liv made me wear a backless dress that clings to my skin everywhere else. I told her I couldn't go out in this, that I wasn't 16 anymore, and she dismissed me, saying I looked hot, and guided me towards a mirror to look at myself. She wasn't wrong, though, the black dress sat against my skin, draping across the chest, and falling just above my knees. If you didn't see my back, it was a pretty modest dress, that I paired with combat boots to balance the sweetness off. I look at myself in the mirror, wipe some fallen mascara off with my fingers, and zhuzh my hair up. I apply a new layer of gloss and let the hand drier blow down my back and neck. When I'm ready, I open the restroom door, and it's as if someone told Alexa to increase the volume to 20.

Making my way back, I feel someone hold my wrist and I look back. It's a guy with a smile on his face, he mouths, "Wanna dance?".

I kinda do, I think to myself. My friends are here somewhere, so I don't feel unsafe, and it's not like I'm going off with him to some back alley. It's just dancing, and there are lots of people here. "Sure!" I yell back at him.

The music is Latin now, so this guy is trying to show me how to properly move my arms and hips to the rhythm. I can't say I'm very good at this, but he seems to know what he's doing, he's guiding and twirling me, making me laugh.

"You're pretty good at this!" I move closer to his ear.

He wraps his arm around my waist and is doing a sort of move where our legs mirror each other, going in the same direction. "Thank you!" he laughs in my ear, "I'm actually Columbian, so you could say it's in my blood!" He smiles wide at me and I can tell he truly loves this.

"I wish I were better at this." I tell him, "To keep up with you!"

"Nah, you're fine, look at you! You haven't stepped on my toes once!"

I grin at his words. He pushes me back, then with a little tug, I'm twirling back into his arms, and he drops us, holding me against him and secure on his arm. The music ends, "Wow! That was amazing!" I put my hands on his shoulders and jump up and down, excited that he made me look cool. I give him a swift hug, thanking him, and that's when I feel a tap on my shoulder.

I turn around and am welcomed by stormy, green eyes. "I think it's time to go."

My whole body wants to lurch at him immediately. Who does he think he is, coming in here out of nowhere, interrupting my dance. Before I can say anything, though, the guy behind me, shouts, "Yo, man, I know you! You're Knox Noah, I love the Bears, man!"

Clueless, as most would be in the presence of a star, he doesn't read the room. Fed up with how everyone instantly loves him, *without* actually knowing him, I leave them both and turn towards the bar. I need a drink, *stat.*

I haven't even taken more than six steps when I feel him come up behind me. I roll my eyes at no one; this is what I get for living in a freaking small town with one club for a few thousand people.

He grabs my shoulder, forcing me to turn around, facing him. "What!" I yell at him, crossing my arms against my chest.

"Do you want a drink?" He shouts back.

Blindsided, I say "Yes!" then quickly add, "But not with you!"

I can see a smirk playing across his lips, so I cross my arms against my chest. "I'll get a drink myself."

Snaking around people, I finally reach the bar and try to flag down the bartender. This place is as busy as it gets, and I suddenly wish Sienna was right here and got someone's attention so I wouldn't have to wait another second around here.

I can feel him right behind me, and that only infuriates me more. We've been playing cat and mouse for too long. Facing him, I ask, "What did you do that for? I was having fun! Which I haven't in a while," I add a beat later.

He's staring at me, smirk still on his lips, "Would you like anything to drink?" He gestures towards the bar.

Admitting defeat, because I really can't continue being around him without some liquid courage, I say, "Get me a vodka soda." And I turn around, so I don't have to look at him and wait for the few seconds it takes before the bartender makes his way towards us.

A couple of minutes later, I'm sipping my vodka soda and he's holding a beer.

"Knox..." I touch his arm, "No more games, please." I look him in the eyes, searching for his understanding, "Why did you stop us? I was having fun!"

He looks torn when he answers, "You know why."

I feel my body flush with desire. I want to touch him, have him hold me and never let go. This back and forth that we keep doing makes me hate how much I still let him and my feelings for him affect my life. I wish they wouldn't. I wish I could finally let go, let *him* go. But I know that not all wishes are granted, and this is one that won't go away easily. I mean, we broke up 4 years, 8 months, 11 days (and a few hours) ago – not that anyone's counting - and I'm still thinking about him. I still let thoughts of him consume me day and night. "I don't know why", I mutter.

He sighs and swipes his hand across his hair. "Look, I guess I have no right to tell you who to dance with or not, but it's still weird, okay?"

"I bet that it's just as weird as seeing you with a different model every week!"

"Since when do you pay attention to what I do? At first, you said you didn't even know anything about my life in Chicago, but now you know that they're models, specifically. Interesting." He eyes me and takes a swig of his beer.

I roll my eyes at him, trying to mask how he caught me red-handed. "I think everyone knows about that." I add a second later, "And Liv told me, actually. I haven't seen a thing."

"Sure thing…", he's feeling pretty cocky now.

"Besides, that didn't answer my question. Why do you care? You're not calling the shots in my life." I try to regain some control of the conversation.

"I know. I've told you why." He takes a step closer to me, making our distance even more suffocating. "I'm sorry."

Changing the subject as quickly as I stopped breathing with him so near, I ask, "So, did you have a good Christmas? Your mom was so happy you were back in town for the holidays."

He looks displeased with my change in topic. "Yep. Pretty good time being back here, all things considered." He grabs his stomach and adds, "Coach is gonna be mad, though, I've probably gained a few pounds and I'd promised I would keep a good regimen here."

"I'm sure you'll be fine." I dismiss his statement with a shrug. "Can't you just go for a run and burn it off?"

He laughs, "Yeah, something like that. I've still been practicing here anyway. We have game after New Year's, so I need to be ready."

"Right…" I don't know what else to add to that. This feels weird, this conversation doesn't feel like it's truly happening. Why do we have to be so cordial with each other and talk about things like the weather and school. It's like things are normal, but they're *not*. We haven't talked in so long, so things shouldn't be like this. That thought reminds me of something. "Did you like my gift?"

He looks bothered by that question and it takes a few seconds before he answers, "I haven't opened it yet actually."

A wave of cold sweat crashes into me, from head to toes. What was I just saying… things are not normal between us, and they really shouldn't be. This is not normal. "So, you want to ignore me when you get into town, then climb up my bedroom window, fight with me, stop me from dancing with another guy, pretend it's all fine and rainbows and then, you actually can't open a freaking gift!?" I raise my voice and myself more, getting closer to his face.

"Look, Triona, I don't have the answers for everything, okay…? But you were the one who went to Chicago a year after we broke up and you didn't tell me you were there. You admitted you went there for me, only now, what… three years too late, and you think I'm supposed to just be okay with everything?" He's hurt. I can see it in his face, the way his eyes are wild in pain, his jaw tense and his voice cracking.

I also feel like a caged animal, wanting to burst free, let everything be finally taken from me, "I don't know what you're supposed to do." I grab his left forearm, "I don't know what *we*'re supposed to do." I shake my head, my eyes drop to the floor, "I did go there for you, Knox. I went there in the hopes of seeing you. I wanted to make sure you were happy. I wanted to find a piece of me that I had lost and couldn't heal anymore."

He grabs me by the wrist, takes me away from the throng of people surrounding us, we move towards the red door, he makes a gesture to someone, and in the next couple of seconds, the door closes behind us, stripping away the loud music.

"I don't think I'll ever get used to this." He looks at me, a question in his eyes. "You. Everyone knowing you and opening doors for you." I gesture towards him and the door a couple of feet from us.

He moves across from me, leaning against the wall. The corridor we're in is only maybe 3-feet wide, but the distance gives me enough space for a deep breath.

"I don't care about those things. It just so happens to be helpful in getting what I want from time to time." He shrugs his shoulders.

"Yeah, I can see that." I put my empty glass on the floor by my feet. "It's still weird, though. You're just Knox to me, you know?" That's how I still see him. Just Knox.

My Knox.

My cheeks blush with that realization. *He's no longer mine*, I tell my brain.

"What were you thinking about just now?" He doesn't miss a beat.

"Nothing much," I lie.

"You always blush when you're embarrassed. Your neck turns into a beet. I know you, remember? Like, truly know you?" The way he's looking at me makes me squirm. I see his eyes navigate through my body, and I need to cross my legs. If I weren't blushing before, he definitely has me turning red now.

He takes a step towards me and pushes my hair away from my neck. "What were you thinking about, Ina?" he whispers in my ear.

I close my eyes, my rapid breathing betraying how collected I'm pretending to be. I scramble for words in my brain, how does one form a sentence, is it normal for a human being to lose all ability to speak from one tiny touch? "You", I manage to mumble.

"You were thinking about me?" He pushes his body flat against mine, forcing me to look up at him. "I'm right here, Ina. You don't have to think about me."

That's all I can take. Before I know it, I crash into his body, my lips meeting his in a frenzy. I wrap my arms around his neck, pull him into me and kiss him like I've been starved for 4 years, 8 months and 11 days, maybe 12 now? What time is it? Oh my God, why am I thinking about what time it is now, mid-kiss?

As if he read my mind, he glides his hands from my waist and squeezes my butt before lifting me and pinning me against the wall. I wrap my legs around his waist, moving my hands across whatever part of his body I can touch now. He pushes into me and I let out a moan. Oh god, someone will hear us outside this corridor. Remembering where we are, I push against his chest, "Wait, wait." His chest is moving erratically, alongside mine. His hands are still on my ass, holding me up. "Knox, wait, put me down."

He looks at me confused, but he immediately lets go of me.

I gently pat my lips with the back of my hand, making sure I don't have lipstick all over my mouth, and I comb through my hair with my fingers. The gestures give me some time to collect myself and my thoughts. "What are we doing, Knox?"

He looks at me, hair disheveled, "I don't know. I guess I can't control my feelings around you. I'm sorry." He shrugs.

"No, I kissed you. *I'm* sorry. I shouldn't have." I bend down to pick up my glass.

"You shouldn't have?" he snickers.

I close my eyes for a second, begging myself to make sense of it all. "No, Knox. We're no longer together, you've let go of me a long time ago, and I shouldn't have kissed you right now. I'm sorry."

A flash of hurt crosses his face. "I've let go of you? You seem to be mistaken. You let go of me." He crosses his arms, back to staring me from where he was.

"Knox…" I sigh, "I really don't think we should discuss this now." I'm ready to leave this corridor and let the music swallow me whole.

"Right. Not now, or ever. Right? After all my calls and texts, you still didn't think it was worth discussing then, so why would it fucking matter discussing it now, right?"

I turn to the door and I'm turning the handle when he grabs me by the shoulder. "Please, stay." He begs me. "Let's talk about this."

"I… can't." I tell him, hoping he feels discouraged enough to just let me go.

"Ina, please. I think we could handle this now. We're older. I've grown a bit…" he mutters.

His hand is splashed against the door that I'm still facing. I can hear his words behind me, I can hear the honesty in his words.

I say the next words staring at the ground, hoping it'll help me feel more in control. "We let each other go, Knox. We broke up with each other, and I really couldn't handle the pain then, so I don't care if you called me a thousand times. I just couldn't let you in again. I knew you'd be focused on football and then your career, and that's it." I don't pause to breathe, fearing I won't be able to say this out loud, "It really doesn't matter anymore. You've moved on. You have your career ahead of you now, just like you've always wanted, and whatever our stupid selves decided 4 years ago doesn't matter anymore." I look at him and ask, "Right?"

He shakes his head, "Whatever. If you say so, then you're right." He moves to the side, gently pushes me away, opens the door and leaves me. Again.

By no fault of anyone other than myself, Knox Noah leaves me again.

Minutes later, after pulling myself together, I make my way out of that doomed corridor and find Sienna and Liv in the VIP section we have for ourselves.

"Hiiiiiiiiiiiiiiii!" Liv jumps at me, clearly very tipsy.

"Hi!" I laugh and give her a side hug. "How're we doing here?"

Sienna responds for her, "She's having a lot of fun! And so am I. Where did you run off to? We saw you with Knox."

"Yes! We saw you with him!" Liv shouts in my face.

"Yeah, he showed up and we talked," I shrug.

Their long faces show me they're waiting for more. "Guys, I wanna have fun with you!" I shake Liv. "I don't wanna talk about him now. Let's dance!" I grab them both by the hand and lead them towards the dance floor.

We spend the next couple of hours swaying to all the latest hits, and at some point, Sienna even asks the DJ to play our favorite song from when we were 14. Spending time with my best friends is really what I needed at the end of a year filled with projects, a lot of studying and way too much TV stalking of a certain someone. Hanging out, dancing away all my troubles is definitely a much better way to end the year, and I hope this feeling can carry me away into the new year. I want to stay focused on school and work hard in my summer internship. Everyone knows it takes around 2 years after graduating to finally become a true architect, with a lot of work and interning in between, so I need to keep my head in the *game*, ironically. I'll feel much lighter after I've finished this period of time in my life.

Sienna stops jumping up and down to an electronic beat, and holds my wrist, pulling me closer, "I really don't want you to leave me here alone again!"

I squeeze her, sharing the same feeling. "I know, me neither, S."

Liv joins in, and we hug each other tightly. We stay in a circle, dancing for a couple more songs, and then decide to take a break and go drink some water in our private booth.

"Wow! I think I've sweated through my shirt completely", Liv points out.

We giggle at her. "I'm definitely sticky!" I reply, fanning my neck.

They're also laughing and then suddenly stop, a serious look on their faces.

I look behind my shoulder and see Knox climbing up the few steps separating the VIP area from the dance floor.

"I'm gonna go to the restroom. Be right back," I tell them and leave without looking in his direction.

Standing in front of the mirror I've stared at twice now, I look at my reflection and wonder how my life got here. I fell in love with a guy that wasn't my type, he got injured and we basically played house for some time, then he gets into a great school that happens to be very far away from where I want to go and the few months we're not in the same town, the long distance breaks us. I spend years regretting my decision, but never tell him so. Where are your fucking ovaries, Triona. I know this is heavier than a usual bullet point list, but stating the facts helps me clear my head. What would any of this matter now, anyway? He's still in Chicago, and I'm still in New Haven. Great making out or not, the truth is we're still far away, and worse, now he has a lot more at stake with his professional career. Things are just not meant to be... Right? I try to convince myself that they aren't. If he wanted the same, he would say so, he wouldn't have agreed with me before.

Right?

I don't know anything anymore. All I know right now is that being back in town has really fucked up with my mind even more than I thought possible.

Pulling my phone out from my pocket, I see that I've been here for over 20 minutes, which is long enough for people to start wondering if I'm passed out in here. I open the door, then hurry through that damned corridor, and I'm back again inside the club. I look at the other corner, searching for Liv and Sienna and I don't see him with them, so I make my way there.

"Guys, I think I'm gonna leave." I shout towards them.

Their faces immediately give me surprised looks, "What? Already? No! We wanna stay longer and dance all night!" Liv shouts back.

"You can stay, I don't want you to have to leave because of me. I just want to go home and sleep."

Sienna looks concerned, "What happened? He just came over to say hi", she explains.

I shrug, "It's okay. I just need to sleep for a few hours before making the long trip. I'll call you tomorrow when I'm driving back."

We all share a hug and I tell them to drink responsibly and that we'll talk soon.

I couldn't get home fast enough, the cab I got into drove me home in record time. I can't believe we made out in a corridor at the back of the club, what are we, 16? For fuck's sake. Before getting into bed, I drink a tall glass of water and change into my pajamas. The few hours of sleep I manage to get are filled with dreams of taps on my window, but when I get up to see who's there, nobody is. In real life, it's all the same, nobody is there.

17.

My alarm goes off at 11am, which I consider late for the long drive I have ahead of me, but also, I needed to get at least 7 hours of sleep, otherwise I'd be falling asleep behind the wheel. With my eyes still closed, I move across my bedroom, and turn the cold water on in the shower. It's dreadful, but I need it to wake up quickly.

I can't say I have done a lot of partying back in New Haven, so maybe I'm not as used to the consequences anymore, but my head is banging and the 2-minute-cold shower only helps a little.

Wrapping myself in a towel, I move swiftly through my closet and throw a few things on my bed, wanting to pack them to take back with me. A few sweaters that I brought will go back with me, plus a couple of leggings that I'd missed wearing. I see a pile of clean laundry, so I grab it all and dump it inside my suitcase too. I'll wear my warmest jacket out and my knee boots to face the snow, so it seems that I have everything I might need. I tidy my room a bit, making the bed and arranging the pillows, folding some other clothes I have lying around and putting them back in the closet. I've also gathered all my toiletries and my suitcase is now ready to go.

Sitting on my bed, I look around what used to be my comfort zone. I spent many nights crying on this bed, talking to Sienna and Liv, texting crushes, and thinking about the future. Now, my bedroom holds those older memories and more recent ones of him climbing up to my window, nights spent watching movies together, and a lot of make out sessions that happened on my bed, and other surfaces. I look over at my closet, the door still open, and I laugh to myself. It reminds me of that one time we thought it would be best to do it inside there to make less noise. I eye the box I stuffed back behind clothes that are now in my suitcase, and my legs walk over without my brain's permission. I rummage through it again, and I find the letter that could've changed everything. I'd stored it here, away from New Haven where it would influence me. I knew it was for the better that when I left after graduation, my summer would start in Yale without this letter, without this option.

I can't explain my next decision, but I put it in my purse. Whatever held me back from bringing it with me 4 and a half years ago doesn't matter anymore. And it makes everything I have accomplished even more special, because it reveals my strength to keep going even when all I wanted to do was to accept it.

Nearly one hour of packing and getting ready got derailed because of my memories, once again. Another reason why I'm better off far away from here, where images of him aren't as clear and deep.

I arrive at the pub a couple of minutes before noon, right on time for the busiest hour before evening beers, so I know I have to make my goodbyes quick. Not only that, but I need to pull this off like a band-aid, otherwise I won't leave.

"Mom, I'm off now." I find her behind the bar, serving a draft beer.

"I know, honey. Do you want me to pack you a sandwich or two for your trip?"

"Oh, yes, please!" I love my mom's sandwiches. "Add extra turkey, please. I'm going inside to say bye to dad." I leave her to finish what she's doing and make my way into the kitchen.

"Hey, dad! You gonna miss me?" I give him a side hug to not interrupt his cooking.

He gets teary-eyed, "Of course I'm gonna miss you, mo stór. You know that." He switches off the gas burner and hugs me tightly.

Mom enters the kitchen and starts making the sandwiches, "Let her be. You know you'll only cry more if you make your goodbye too long", she tells my dad.

"I'll hug her as much as I want to! Don't start with me." He turns to me again and adds, "Honey, please be safe, okay? And come back soon. We want you to visit us here more often. He's not always going to be in town at the same time. Right?" He looks at my mom, waiting for validation.

"That's right. He won't. And you need to show your beautiful face around here more. The ladies at the book club kept asking me if I was sure you hadn't been taken away by the mob." She rolls her eyes, "They're a bunch of silly geese, if you ask me, but they're right, you need to come by more often now. The worst's done."

I know what she means. I missed our town too, and now that I've come back for the first time, I'm sure it'll only get easier. "I know… I promise I'll be back before my internship starts. If all goes well, I'll finish my exams mid-May, so I can come for a couple of weeks before I have to be back there again. Sounds good?"

"Sounds perfect, mo stór!" dad hugs me again and kisses me on the cheek.

"Alright, honey. All done!" mom says while putting the butter knife down. "Here you go." She gives me two foil-wrapped sandwiches and a bag of chips. "Grab yourself a bottle of water and a soda from the fridge if you want."

They walk me to my car, and we hug again before I drop my food and drinks for the road on the passenger's seat and get into the car. "Bye, guys! I'll text you updates from the road, don't worry!" I air-kiss them and turn the engine on. Leaving is always hard, but I have a routine in New Haven to get back to and that will keep my mind off things for a while.

It's been a couple of hours since I first started driving, and I'm feeling ready to take my first break. I hate driving at night, so I want to get there as soon as possible, but I cannot drive non-stop just for the sake of getting there before nightfall. I left too late this morning anyway, so there's no way I'd be there before midnight, not even counting the breaks I'll take along the way. My brain's already tired of counting cars, looking at the landscape passing by, and I've probably planned a to-do list in my head 5 different times, all just to keep myself busy and distracted. But I literally have nothing else to think of, and playing music only seems to strengthen the thoughts I want to avoid.

Thinking about last night and replaying our conversation in my head, I realize that if I hadn't stopped us, we probably would have continued what we started and gone back to his parents'. I feel my body tense up at the thought, and I push it away. I can't let myself think this way anymore. I know I'm the one who shut things down, and I realize now that he's been imploring me to be honest with him about certain things, but I can't switch off the part of me who's afraid. If it didn't work out before, why would it now; if he wants to find out about the past, what guarantees he won't be upset by my choices; if I'd let us be intimate again last night, what would prevent him from leaving for Chicago and never speak to me for another 4 years… There are so many questions, concerns and doubts that assault me every time I try to feel braver and just tell him. I cannot switch these off. I've tried… I let some of it go last night. Kissing him again made me lose my mind for a few seconds, but then these questions crashed into my sould again, and I couldn't see anything other than my pain from over 4 years ago.

After a few more hours on the road, a shameful number of tears and a couple more breaks, I decide to distract myself with Sienna and Liv and call them up on our group chat.

Liv answers after the first ring, "Hey, gorgeous, what's up? Where are you now?"

I smile at her through the camera, "Hey, yourself. I'm halfway there, kinda. What were you up to? Not too hangover?"

"Shit, way too hangover. S wanted us to do shots after you left. I threw it all up before falling asleep on my bedroom floor. I woke up this morning cold and sore." She laughs.

"You guys went hard then. I only woke up with a headache, but I took an aspirin and that fixed it. Where's S? She's not answering."

"No clue. She put me in a cab and said she had a ride home later. I left her around 5, so I have no idea who could've picked her up at that time," she tells me.

"We really have to demand for an update soon, she's been sneaking around. D'ya think she's going out with someone from the club? I mean, she knew people there. That would explain it." I shrug, hoping she can see me, as I can't look down at my phone while driving.

"Yeah, guess so… I'll interrogate her when I see her again tomorrow. We're going to meet up with some people who were at the bonfire for New Year's. Someone's house, but don't know whose."

"Oh, that sounds like fun. Maybe you can see Matt again?" I wiggle my eyebrows.

I hear her laugh sarcastically. "I'll have you know he shot me down, so I don't think we'll be seeing each other again soon. He hurt my ego…" I can hear in her voice that she's making it sound like it's nothing, but I've never heard her say something like that, so I'm momentarily worried about her.

"I'm sure he just didn't know what to say to you… He was always a bit timid in high school, even though he always had people wanting to date him when he became QB in our senior year, remember?"

"Sure… I remember." I hear some rustling. "Anyway, how are you feeli-"

I hear a ping that tells me Sienna joined our group call. "Finally! Where were you?" Liv immediately asks her.

"None of your business. Hey, Tee, how are you doing today?" She changes her focus to me.

Before I can answer her, Liv asks again, "None of my business? Are you out of your mind? You could've sent me a text at least. I was worried sick about you!"

"I'm sure you probably woke up like an hour ago, don't be so dramatic, Liv." Sienna tells her. "But anyway, I told you I had a ride. I just got back home now, so I was gonna text you, but saw you guys were talking, so even better! I'm here now."

After about half an hour of Liv bombarding Sienna with more questions about her love life and who she spent the night with, they both decide to call it a tie and move on to another topic that's been on their minds, it seems.

"Tee, what happened yesterday with Knox?" Sienna asks me.

"Yeah, you promised you'd share with us… I've been thinking about it all day!" Liv adds.

"Surely not all day, Liv. But yeah… I guess I should tell you now so you can keep me company for a bit longer."

"We'd stay on the line with you either way, but yes, we're dying to know!" Liv responds excitedly.

I can hear a door closing and some more rustling, so I can only assume they're both sitting in their bedrooms, waiting to hear my news.

"So, we kissed." I choose to be straight to the point.

They both screech through the phone, making me want to laugh at how giddy they still get about anything Knox-related. "*Gurls*, calm down. I know this may sound exciting, but things ended poorly again. We kissed, I mean, *I* actually kissed him…" some more screaming from them, I continue when they can hear me again, "And then I had a total freak out moment and I stopped it."

"What! Why?", these come from Sienna.

"I just don't know anymore. What if he hooked up with me last night and then we never spoke again?"

They tut. "I don't think that would happen, Tee", Liv tells me.

"Me neither…" Sienna agrees.

"Maybe not, but you know how I get. I overthought that moment, I got scared… I feel like I had to overcome so much when we broke up. I don't think I could do the same now. I have to focus on finishing my degree and my internship starts in a few months, I can't afford to be distracted by how miserable I would feel if things didn't go according to plan", I explain to them.

"But what would the plan be exactly?" Liv asks me.

I shrug my shoulders, "I wish I knew. I really do. But I don't."

"Oh, c'mon, Tee. Enough's enough. You know what you want, you may be afraid of it and not want to say it out loud, but you freaking know", Sienna surprises me by saying.

I find myself speechless, so she continues, "Tee, we love you, but you've been lying to yourself for far too long. You guys broke up when you were both young. And you know he tried to make it right, so why do you keep fighting it? Why are you so afraid of actually trying?"

Tears pool in my eyes and I have to take a deep breath before replying, "I don't want to slow him down…"

Silence invades my car for a few seconds, both of them taking time to process my words and feelings.

Liv speaks first, "Tee, I don't think we're the ones who you need to hear this from, but I'm 110% positive Knox would never think you'd be slowing him down. What do you mean?"

"I don't know…" I use the back of my hand to wipe a few tears that slid down my cheeks. "I guess that when we broke up, I just thought it would be easier that way. I had Yale and the summer school still had available spots, and when I left, I convinced myself that long distance would be too difficult for us. We literally had never spent time apart, you know? When he left that January, we would speak every night at first. He sent me photos every few hours, a million texts every day and we were still really *on* it. We were physically apart, but we were compensating by the amount of time we spent FaceTiming. But then, his practices became harder, and longer. His coach told him she'd like to have him start as quarterback in the new school year, that he would have to work harder but that it would put him in front of the people who mattered. She had his back, I'm not saying he should've done anything differently. But that meant we spent less and less time texting, or FaceTiming. Just before we broke up, we both had an intense couple of weeks. It was finals' week for us three, and he had a couple of important games that would take him off the bench for the first time, potentially. We just didn't speak for those two weeks." I stop for a minute or so, thinking back to that time and how challenging those weeks had been for me, not having him there next to me, cheering me on as he'd always done. Sienna and Liv are still quiet, waiting for me to continue.

"We had a stupid fight after that, and we decided we couldn't do long distance anymore. We had to focus on each of our futures. You know, he didn't really start contacting me again until over a month later, so by that time, I truly believed it had been for the better. And I knew he needed to be the starting quarterback to get a shot at an NFL career, and with their former QB graduating, I knew he'd get it in the new school year, after the summer. So, I left things as they were... I actually blocked his number when I got to New Haven because I didn't trust myself to not answer him", I shrug again, thinking about how that had seemed the easiest solution at the time for a while.

"I just thought he'd be focused on his career, and I would only be a distraction, you know? He had almost lost it all with his injury, I didn't want to be in his way," I finish.

"Wow...", Liv mutters.

I can hear one of them gulp loudly. "I'm sorry you had to believe that for this long, Tee", Sienna says. "I hope you see now that maybe that should've been his decision to make. And the way I remember it, when he came back that summer before college started again, he would have undoubtedly disagreed with you. Maybe things weren't supposed to work out back then, you both had some growing to do, and maybe that growing apart taught you things you can use now. You know, do differently."

"Maybe...", I manage to say.

"You know, we told him you were leaving today and he seemed hurt", Liv says.

"Last night at the club", Sienna explains.

"Yeah, I figured… I'm sure he'll be okay, though. He agreed with me when I told him the past didn't matter now. He'll be with a new model next week, you'll see…" That thought makes me die a little inside, but I hope it's true. I hope I'll see him on the tabloids and maybe that will be the extra kick I need to close this chapter… *damn*, this whole book, really.

After chatting a little about New Year's and their plans, we hang up and I'm left alone with my thoughts again. If he wanted, and cared, he would have texted me. He could have said something right after the club, maybe this afternoon even. But he didn't, and that speaks more than words.

When I finally get to campus, it's past 2 in the morning, but I still shoot a quick message to my parents and in our group to tell everyone I've arrived safe and sound. Wrapping myself under my duvet, the fatigue hits me all of a sudden and thoughts of him don't have time to consume me, I'm asleep in under five minutes.

18.

The next morning, or shall I say afternoon, I wake up after a long, well-deserved sleep and check my phone. I have a missed call from my mom, who probably thought I'd be up before noon, and a few messages to read in our group chat. I quickly return my mom's call to let her know I'm doing okay and finally up, and to ask her about dad. When we hang up, I get the courage to get out of bed and decide to keep myself busy this afternoon with errands and cleaning up my dorm room. I feel very privileged to still live on campus as most graduates would need to find a place to live off-campus, and most would prefer it, but I love being able to walk around the building at night and feel like I could meet new people every semester.

I answer a couple of emails sent by a professor and start working on my extracurricular project I want to hand in before the new semester begins. A couple of hours go by and when my neck starts to feel stiff, I get up from my desk and decide to unpack my suitcase. I make two piles on my bed, one to wash, the other to put away. I feel lucky I used my parent's washing machine after Christmas, so I don't have a lot of laundry to do. I still decide to take the unwashed pile to the laundry room, seeing as most students are not back from their hometowns yet, and I won't have to wait for a machine to become available. Sure enough, there's no one in the laundry room, so I start my load and go back upstairs to tidy up the rest of my room while the machine is on. I put away the other pile of clothes, folding them nicely and putting them in a chest of drawers I have by the door, and hanging whatever needs to be wrinkle-free. I find my black belt, which must have been in the middle of the pile I threw inside my suitcase back at home, so I roll it up and put it by my socks.

Another hour goes by, I've finally finished tidying everything up, and I'm about to call Liv and Sienna to find out what they're up to.

"Hi, did you miss us already?" Liv answers the phone asking.

"Hey, Tee!" Sienna answers on the first ring this time too.

"Hey, best friends! What are you up to?", I lay on my bed, legs dangling over the mattress.

"Oh god, what's up with you?" Liv inquires.

"Nothing's up with me, don't be mean. I'm just bored and I want to live vicariously through you. Tell me, tell me!"

"Well, we're meeting in a couple of hours to get ready together to go out to Matt's house for New Year's," Sienna tells me.

"Matt's house?" I shout into the phone.

I can *hear* Liv rolling her eyes. "Yeah! Didn't Liv tell you?" Sienna asks.

"No! She did not say it was *Matt's* house. Liv…?"

"Who cares whose house it is? A bunch of us are gonna go, so we might not even see him," Liv remarks.

"Sure…", I say unconvinced. "Bet you left that out on purpose, Ms. Moralis!" I tease her.

"Whatever…" is all she says.

"I never took you for shy, Liv. Why are you all of a sudden hiding something about this?" I ask her.

"I'm really *not*. You guys are just making things up. You are the ones who believe there's something here, when there's not. And I told you he shot me down. I didn't know it was his house."

"Okay, okay, don't get mad, I'm sorry," I apologize to her.

"Yeah, whatever," she responds. "What about you? What are you doing tonight?"

"You know… gonna have the best time of my life. I'm throwing a huge party, get some alcohol up here, probably some jazz on to get the mood right... All for me, myself and I," I say sarcastically.

"Booo, you're such a lame-o sometimes", Liv throws at me.

"Oww, honey, I agree with Liv on this. Isn't there a party somewhere on campus you could go to?" Sienna asks.

"Yeah, I'm sure there is. I actually heard some girls talk about a party off-campus they're going to, but honestly, I just feel like staying here and getting a good night's sleep, guys."

"On New Year's Eve? Really!?"

"Liv, we can't always be up for a good time. I just need to lick my wounds, get a nice glass of wine and watch a TV show. I'm gonna be watching the live countdown, though, so I'm still gonna be thinking about you at midnight, don't worry!" I tease her.

"God, we shouldn't have let you go up there by yourself. At least you'd go out with us tonight if you'd waited a couple more days," Sienna comments in a whisper.

"Guys, I'm fine. Really. I just had to come back. I've spent the afternoon thinking about other things, I'm good here. It's helping me forget," I confess to them.

"I get it... I still think you're a lame-o, but I get it. Just don't spend the night watching old interviews of him. I'm sure you have a folder saved just for those sweaty videos of him, you naughty, naught girl!" Liv mocks me.

"I do *not*!" I feel defensive, "Well, maybe I downloaded one or two... but I don't have them in a specific folder - *ha*!"

"She says, thinking that's any better", Liv continues, taunting me.

"Okay, guys, who cares... Stop it. Tee, are you okay, then? Should we be worried?" Sienna's concern warms my heart.

"I'm fine, S. I'll be fine..."

We hang up a while later and I realize I need to start believing my words. I will be fine. I decide to spend another couple of hours working on my project as I don't have much else to do after getting my laundry from the drying machine, and that time flies by. When I notice the time, it's after 8pm, and I set the mood for the night. I connect my phone to the speaker I have on my chest of drawers, choose a soft jazz playlist on Spotify and switch on the fairy lights hanging on the wall above my bed. I open a bottle of white wine I had in my mini-fridge and serve myself a full glass since I won't be going out tonight.

Grabbing my Kindle, I click on the latest book I was reading before I left for the holidays, and I immediately regret my decision. I had stopped at a scene where the main character is on her knees, hands tied behind her back, and her friend is about to use a violet wand on her nipples for the first time. I click off the book right away, not wanting certain thoughts to make me think about him yet again.

Maybe I should *really* turn my words real. I never thought I'd do this, but picking up my phone from my side table, I open the play store and decide to do the unthinkable: I download Tinder. Give a girl a break, okay? I need to start dating again, and the singles night just wasn't doing it for me. Tinder, it is. Am I going to regret it? Most likely… But what else am I supposed to do?

Not even a couple of minutes later, I'm already bored and quit trying to fill out my profile. I don't know what to write, I don't know what photos to upload, and it just feels like a difficult task for tonight. Also, who is out there swiping on New Year's Eve?

Scratch that… I guess many people are, actually.

I grab my laptop instead, cozying up on the bed under my duvet, glass of wine in my hand, and I pull up my favorite TV show that gets me through anything. I'm two episodes in when I start getting hungry and this wine has definitely gone up to my head, with an empty stomach and all, so I walk over to the dorm's shared kitchen and microwave some popcorn. I hope no one comes here right now, I would look pretty pathetic all alone on New Year's Eve, but hey, whatever. I'm turning 23 soon, and I can do whatever I want. Maybe I have someone in my dorm. They don't know that.

Closing the door behind me, unscathed by my nightly stroll, I drop on my bed again and continue watching some more episodes.

'I smell snow…', she says on my laptop screen and the rest of the line is interrupted by my alarm, which I set for 11:50, so I wouldn't miss the chance of ringing in the New Year. I mean, I might be all alone, but I can at least wait for midnight to cheers the new year, hope for new beginnings and something great. I'm watching the live countdown in Times Square and the camera keeps panning on different couples who seem to be too in love and happy to celebrate with hundreds of thousands of strangers around them.

'Ugh!' to all of you happy couples. The ball drops, everyone cheers and kisses, and I take a large gulp of my wine.

I shoot a quick text to my parents wishing them a happy New Year with another promise to visit them soon. I also message Sienna and Liv in our group telling them I miss them and love them, and that the new year will bring amazing things to all of us. Whether I believe my own words or not, the jury's still out on that, but it's past midnight, I'm cozy in my pajamas and ready to sleep. It doesn't take me long to fall asleep while still watching a show on my laptop.

I wake up to knocks that sound more like banging. I wonder for a few seconds if I had a little too much to drink with that bottle of wine.

Knock.

Knock-knock.

It's clearly not in my head. I feel around my bed, searching for my phone and when I light it up, I see it's 4 in the morning. Probably some student who had a little too much to drink and doesn't know where their dorm is.

'Argh', I lay back in bed, hoping whoever it is will give up and go away.

Knock-knock-knock.

Silence.

Knock.

Then I hear it.

"Ina… are you there?"

It's him.

Knox is here.

Am I ready now?

19.

I open the door, not trusting my ears. I need to see him to believe it. As soon as my eyes adjust to the light in the corridor, I see him. It is him. He's standing against the door frame, one arm above his head, holding onto the wall. My heart is beating a thousand miles per minute and my throat is suddenly dry.

"What are you doing here?" I say, my voice shaky.

"Can I come in, please?" he looks at me with such intensity that I cannot do anything other than give him a quick nod.

I switch on the lamp on my desk to make this moment a little less nerve wracking, but also to not bother us with too much brightness. I sit on my bed then, one leg crossed under my butt. My hands are twitching around, I still don't know what to say.

He saves me by starting, "I like your room." His eyes follow along my walls with the fairy lights above my bed and photos randomly placed, the bed where I'm sitting unmade with my laptop still on it, a plant by the window on my desk and a few other decorations I've accumulated over the years here. "It's cozy." He pulls my desk chair and sits, facing the back of the chair, forearms hanging from the top.

"Yeah… it's small but I like it." I'm momentarily distracted by him pushing his sweater back on his forearms.

He's staring at me now, the back of the chair facing my bed. "You left…"

I look down at my hands, playing with my pants' string. I don't know what to tell him. It feels like he's been listening to my inner thoughts and had to come over to get me to say them to him out loud. An unexpected desire to open myself up to him, to tell him all my fears and everything that happened on my side when we broke up fills me.

"What are you doing here, Knox?", I ask instead.

"You left without saying anything. After the club."

"And you could've also said something if you wanted to. You could've messaged me", I argue back.

He pauses then, mulling over his next words, I'm sure. "Triona, I didn't come all the way here to fight again. I want to have a real conversation with you. I want us to be real and honest with each other. Okay? Do you think we can do that?" His voice is soft and pleading. I can see he's serious about this. Can I give that to him? Am I ready to open this wound further again?

"Okay…", I whisper.

His eyes seem to light up with my acceptance. He stands up and instructs me, "I have an idea to make this easier for you, and for me. Do you trust me?" I move my head downwards an inch. "Okay, sit right here." He leads me to the floor, against my bed footboard. "I'll sit on this side, so we're not facing each other, but I'm still right here." He sits down on the floor as well, but against the side rail. He's still so close, I could touch him if I reached to my right.

"Now, close your eyes… I'll close mine too." I close my eyes as he says and hear him moving around to get comfortable.

"Done…", I tell him.

"Okay." He takes a deep breath in and exhales through his mouth. "I'm gonna start. But the way we do this is we have to be 100% honest, no hiding anything even if whatever it is could hurt the other one. And you cannot jump to any conclusions. If we have any doubts or questions about anything, we need to ask the other, simple as that. Deal?"

"Okay…", I mutter, my voice still shaky.

"Oh, and we cannot interrupt each other. I'll let you finish, no matter how long it could take. And you'll do the same for me." He explains.

"Okay…", I repeat.

My nerves are shot right now. I wondered for so long if I should've been honest with him, if I should take my chances and tell him the truth, let him take it all away from me and do with it whatever he pleased. Whenever I thought of it, though, I'd grow even more ashamed. I could not unload on someone who didn't deserve it. Someone who had so much going on for him already, it wasn't his duty to hear me out and deal with my own guilt. But he's asking now… He's been asking for some time, if I'm honest with myself. And I feel ready… *I think.*

"I'm sorry I didn't say anything to you at the pub", he starts, "I wasn't expecting to see you in town because everyone told me you had never gone back. I felt so angry all of a sudden. You had never said anything to me, and I got so angry at everything again. I didn't want to feel that way, but that's how I felt." He pauses for a few seconds before continuing, "I went to my parents' home that night and everywhere I looked you were there. My bedroom *is* you", he sighs. "The anger slowly turned into sadness, and I was back at the end of my first semester, after we broke up, not knowing what was happening, what I should do, if I should do anything at all…"

"I'd missed you so badly. It hurt to see you because my feelings never changed. It was like fire burned through my whole body and I only connected it to anger for how things ended, but it was also the realization that my love for you has remained the same. I tried to fight it, you know… I went on dates in my second year at college. The team always had girls around, it wasn't hard to pick one and ask her on a date."

Hearing that stings, but I control myself and let him speak. I need to hear his side and understand what was going on in his life. I need to hear his words to make sense of mine.

"I felt sorry for myself for still being hung up on you after so long. I thought you'd have moved on too, and you'd want nothing to do with me. So when I saw you at the bonfire, I felt like hurting you a little." He moves beside me and I hear him swallow loudly. "I'm not proud of that. But seeing you again there, having fun, I just couldn't handle how I was hurting and you seemed just fine. It looked like you didn't even care that it had been the first time seeing me just a few days before. So, I said what I said… And I regretted it immediately. I saw the hurt in your face, Ina. I was happy to notice you hadn't changed too much. I can still see and read your facial expressions easily." He laughs sarcastically. "But I knew I'd hurt you and that made me want to throw up. I went looking for you again later, but you had already left. So I went to you. That part you already know…", he exhales.

"Do you wanna tell me what's your perspective on all of this?" he asks me.

I nod, but then remember we still have our eyes closed. "Er- yeah… I can do that." I take some time to think about how I can share these vulnerable things to him. "I guess I was also upset with you. I don't know how to do this." I gesture between us, realizing, again, he cannot see me. "I don't know how I should act, what I should say. I didn't know if you even remembered me", I shrug my shoulders.

"Wha-?" he stops himself. "Sorry, continue."

"I know it may sound crazy, my rational side also tells me it's not like you would forget me, or us. But there's also a part of me that feeds me these doubts, and I just didn't know what to do. I was surprised you didn't come over to our table to, at least, say hi to Sienna and Liv, but then I thought you were maybe too deep in your stardom." Before he can protest again, I add, "I know you're not, Knox. It's just hard to debate against yourself. I had all kinds of thoughts running through my mind for days. And when you still didn't say anything to me at the bonfire, I felt like that was truly the end. That you would never speak to me again. And in a way, I didn't blame you. I had been the one to not answer your calls and messages, so why would you even wanna speak to me now, anyway. Right? That's how it felt to me…"

"So, why did you lie to me about Chicago that night in your kitchen?"

I jerk my shoulders and arms. "I don't know, Knox. It's not easy to open up like that. And I didn't think it would matter to tell you now, like almost 4 years later, that I had gone there to see you. I didn't even know at the time that I was really there for you. I convinced myself that you weren't the sole purpose of my being there."

After a few seconds, he asks, "Why didn't you tell me at that time you were there, though?"

"I was waiting for a sign…", I confess. "I know it sounds stupid, but you had stopped messaging me. I had your number blocked for a while, so I don't even know if you were trying to contact me at the beginning, but then you were, and then you stopped. I didn't know if you had a girlfriend neither. I didn't know if you even wanted to see me again. So, I waited for a sign that I should call you. I thought maybe I would just meet you in the middle of the street. That would've been a really good sign…" I laugh quietly.

I hear him sigh, "Yeah… that would've been pretty epic… Maybe it'd have fixed things then."

"I don't know if that's true, Knox," I tell him.

"Why?" he simply asks.

"We were still long distance. That hadn't worked for us very well. I think it could have made things worse if we'd tried again."

"Maybe." I can hear the defeat in his voice.

"But we're being candid with each other now, right? That could help?" I try to cheer him up. Myself too, if I'm honest. "Maybe you can tell me why you're here right now? What made you come all the way here?"

"I saw you leave the club. Once again, Triona Gallagher is running away, I thought. I was hurt again, Tee. You kiss me, then regret it. Later I come to find out you're leaving the next day, and you never even thought of telling me. It all felt too familiar. It feels like we've going around in circles all these years, and these last few days we had a front row seat to our own little circle show. I just couldn't understand why you kept pushing me away. Kept running away from me. Then, yesterday, when I woke up in the afternoon, I saw your gift. I was packing and it was just there, sitting on my windowsill. I opened it and it took my breath away, Ina", he pauses to clear his throat. "I thought to myself, if she has moved on, why did she get me this now? Something that represented our relationship, all the plans we made laying on my truck bed, stargazing, you still remembered them all. You had to. And that had to mean something. Right?" he asks no one in particular.

"I didn't know what to do for a few hours after. I had a plane to catch to Chicago, today in a few hours actually, but I knew I had to see you before. I had to make you talk to me. So, I did what I thought was what would help me out the most, I drove to Sienna's. She told me everything… She said she'd ask for your forgiveness later, but she believed it had been too long for us to still be stuck here, and that it was time we figure it all out. Whatever the outcome would be."

I don't know what to feel about this. I don't blame her for telling him what she knows, but I still don't know what *that* is exactly. He clears it for me next.

"Ina, how could you ever think you'd slow me down? I wanted you to be with me, hell, I'd have gone wherever you wanted to go. I would never think you would be in my way, just like I hope you wouldn't feel that way about me, neither."

Tears are streaming down my face now, and I use both my hands to wipe them away. I feel my heart constrict, and I've been imagining this conversation for so long that I don't expect to feel this way. I thought a weight would lift off my chest, but I just feel like crying harder.

"Ina…" I hear him move closer to me now, and he pulls me onto his lap and wraps his arms around me. "Please don't cry," he whispers against my forehead.

After a few moments of silence and once my crying has evened out, I look at his green eyes and ask him, "Why didn't you tell me this before? You never asked me to move closer to you…"

"You were meant for Yale, Tee. I couldn't ask you to move to Chicago with me. I thought you'd ask me to change schools and be near *you*."

"Ox, I could never ask you that… You fought so hard to get accepted into a school after your injury. I couldn't ask you to change your whole life for me."

"I'd have done anything for you…" he mutters, staring into my eyes.

Remembering something, I get up from his lap and walk towards my door. "Where are you going?" he asks me, worry wrapping his voice. I grab my purse and get what I was looking for inside. Walking back towards him, I sit on the floor, right next to him.

"Here. Open it." I give him the letter that could've changed it all. I know now that it probably would have because of what he just told me.

20.

"What? What is this?" he asks me while unfolding the piece of paper I've just given him.

"Just open it, Ox…", I plead him. Wrapping my arms around my legs, I hold my breath, hoping this won't have disastrous consequences now.

"What does this… Is this what I think it is?" I can't tell by looking at his face if he's upset or not.

Careful, I confess to him, "I hope this shows you that I was also ready to do anything for us, to make a future for us."

He stares at me, looking speechless, and I still don't know if he's upset to find this out only now.

His next move surprises me. He kneels in front of me, throws the letter on my bed, and dives into me, grabbing my face with his two hands and kissing me deeply. When I come up for air, I laugh at him and ask, "Does this mean you're not mad at me?"

"Mad? Wha-? Of course I'm not mad…", he pauses for a second, hands still squeezing my face. "I wish we had been more open with each other back then. I think we both wanted and needed the same things, and we were just too stubborn to admit them. But why would I be mad…? This proves that you wanted me…"

I stare into his eyes, confused at his words. "I've always wanted you, Oxie… That was never the question. So, you're not mad I didn't tell you this before?"

He exhales near my face, "No, Ina. I'm not mad."

"Good…", I whisper.

"Did you really consider going to Chicago?"

"Yeah, of course. As soon as you got confirmation they wanted you for the spring semester, I applied there too. Their architecture program is really good too," I smile at him. "Plus, you were there…", I blush.

"God, I can't believe you were thinking of ditching your Yale future for me." He sits back on his feet. "Did you know I wanted to change schools too? After that semester in Chicago?"

"Actually, yes. But in my defense, I only found out 2 days ago when Sienna and Liv admitted you had gone back into town and talked to them. They had never told me…"

"Fuck, I thought you knew. That messed me up even more. I thought they'd tell you the minute I left and that you chose not to message me, that it hadn't mattered to you." He shakes his head, most likely remembering that time and the 'what ifs' that are also in my head now. "Things could have been so different…"

"I've never stopped thinking about you, Ox… I couldn't. Our break-up was so hard for me because I just didn't get it. Of course long distance is not easy, I knew that, but I never thought that would be the end of our story." I grab his hand in mine, sensing that this conversation needs physical touch and comfort. "Once it happened, it was easy to convince myself that it would be for the best. You hadn't ever mentioned to me that we should go to the same college, so I didn't think that was what you wanted. And I truly believed you would reach your goals faster without having me as a distraction. You know, the toll of dating long distance is a heavy one, and I thought you would spread yourself too thin." I look at him, searching for understanding in his eyes. "I saw how much you worked those months before your surgery, and even more so after the surgery. I had never seen someone try so much, work so hard to be better. To recover. I couldn't be in the way of that…", I explain.

He uses his thumb to wipe a tear that has escaped from my eye. "I hope you know that I have always seen you as my strength. I worked hard to recover because you were there with me every day, cheering me on, and motivating me to want to feel better. You were my motivator. The reason why I would wake up and go to my sessions. I would dream about the times I would be able to take you out again, drive my truck to your house to pick you up, take you to the Swing, go skinny-dipping at the lake. I used these memories to keep me going. *You* kept me going…" He pulls me closer to him, in between his legs. "If you still don't believe this now, please let me convince you of it every single day. Let me come back into your life and prove to you that you'll only be in my way when I'm taking us both to bed, me carrying you in my arms. And, please, let me show you, every second of every day, how much I love you, and how much I need you in my life. Past, present and future, Ina."

I decide to put all doubts and worries I might have aside, and put my hands around his neck, pulling him closer. I brush my fingers against his face, remarking how handsome he is, how in love I am with this man. I let those thoughts, and him, consume me and I cannot wait any longer. I kiss him. His lips are the perfect mix of soft and firm, and he welcomes mine with passion. Soon, I'm being lifted onto his lap and our kisses intensify, our bodies mingling with each other.

"I love you 3001, Knox," I whisper against his ear when he's peppering me with hot kisses against my neck.

He stops for a breath to assure me, "I love you 3002, Ina".

A long session of *(re-)*exploring each other later, we're both laying on my bed, sharing stories and moments from the past 4 years. We have a lot to catch up, but we're taking our time to enjoy each other's presence again. Things have changed, we're both older and more experienced… Knox told me he learned a lot in the locker room from his teammates' stories. I agreed that he clearly knew a new thing or two. But I also love how we're still the same people. He still has a dimple on his right cheek that makes an appearance when he's a little shy about something, he still tells his stories like a philosopher would, and his questions are just as complex and meaningful as they were.

I hope he still sees in me things that made him fall in love with me at first. But I am excited about learning everything else there is to learn. Maybe love isn't about being easy or difficult, and relationships aren't supposed to be smooth-sailing, but it's the curiosity and quiet companionship you find in the other person that makes things work. I can't wait to find out what we are like in a year or two… Maybe even a decade into the future.

"She was so excited, she literally peed herself, Ina!" He laughs hysterically next to me.

"Don't make fun of your mom. I love her!" I scold him.

"But, babe, she had to change her trousers at the airport! How could you not laugh at that?" He's still laughing, holding his stomach.

"It was her lifelong dream!" I explain, "She was so happy you took them there. She even told me about it at the pub, you know? She had stars in her eyes talking about it."

When he finally stops laughing, he says, "Yeah, it was one of the first things I could do for them, and it made me proud to be able to do it."

"Hey! I just remembered, I was also invited to that trip, you know? When are you taking me to Hawaii, Mr. Hotshot?" I tease him.

"I'll take you anywhere you want, babe." He circles his arms around my back, and pulls me against his body, grabbing my ass.

We start making out again, and I can already see we won't want to leave this bed for a few days. If only that was possible… That makes my think about everything we still have to discuss, so much to figure out.

He probably senses a shift in my behavior because his next words are, "What's up, Ina? What are you thinking about now?"

I sigh, "I don't know… Just thinking about all this. Us. What's the plan? Don't get me wrong, I'm really happy you came here and we made up. But we still haven't talked about what's next for us. How can we make this work?" I shrug. "I mean, do you want to make this work?"

"Of course, I do. Look, I haven't thought beyond tonight… I didn't know if you'd even wanna talk to me, so I wasn't cocky enough to think of a plan further than convincing you to finally see me and hear me out."

A smile escapes my lips, "That definitely worked out, though… You have some good planning tactics, I see."

He squeezes me around the waist. He seems to ponder for a few seconds before a smile crosses his whole face. "I think that number one is, do you want to be my girlfriend again, Triona Gallagher?"

Blushing for the tenth time, I mutter, "That's not a question, Knox… You know it's always been yes for me."

"Done! Shall we kiss to make it official?" He wastes no time and kisses me, teeth and all since I'm still laughing.

Then he stops again, and reassures me in a way I didn't know would mean so much to me. "Ina, we're going to fight this time, alright? I only have a couple more months in the season, and we can make plans for me to come to New Haven. I can stay here with you until the summer." I nod at him, having a plan helps me to see things clearer. "And we'll work on our communication this time. We promised that to each other, right? Be honest, be open with each other."

I nod again, trying to whisper to my heart that we have a long road ahead of us, but that we are older and wiser, and we will work on it together.

Another hour later, I hear his stomach growl. "Are you hungry?" I ask him.

He shrugs, "I could definitely eat."

"Should we get some food?" I look at the time, "It's already 7. There must be something open at this time."

His eyes salivate. "Let's go for pancakes!"

I laugh at him and with a shake of my head, say, "Sure, I could eat some pancakes. Let me just get ready. 2 minutes and we're off!"

He distracts himself by looking around my things, "Hey! Isn't this your great, lucky belt?" he asks, his hand still inside my socks' drawer.

"Hey, what about some privacy? What if I was hiding something there?" I joke with him.

"Do you wanna wear it for me?", he wiggles his eyebrows.

Thinking about its meaning and everything I went through while wearing it, I decide it's time for it to go. Its lucky days are definitely over, and I'm ready to make my own luck these days. "Nah, throw it in the trash", I tell him, feeling empowered.

"Sure, babe," he says before moving closer to the one I keep by my bed. "Be gone, sucker!" he says at it.

I'm just changing into a sweater when I can feel him staring at me. "What?" I ask.

He circles the bed, running towards me, and lifts me into the air. I squeal in surprise, and he whispers against my ear, "Let me help you with that."

Epilogue

4 years, 11 months and 22 days later

The lights along main street welcome us home, and my body hums with excitement for being back in town.

"Call me when you want to come over, babe. I'll be back here in 10." He leans over between the two seats, and gives me a quick kiss on the lips. "Love you," he smiles.

"I'll miss you," I pout at him.

He chuckles and pulls me over to him, kissing me again so I won't forget how much he loves me.

"I guess that'll help," I tease him. "I'll call you later then! Have fun."

We say goodbye again, and this time, I actually leave the car. The black door that I've used time and time again greets me with a familiar creak and chime. A waft of hot air and warm food invades me, and I instantly feel right at home. Gallagher's has this power within me, the orchestra of clattering and clinking recognizable to me even with my eyes closed. I can't wait to surprise my parents. They don't know we decided to come back, and I just know they'll both be thrilled we're here this year. Knox only has a couple of days before he has to go back to Chicago for a game, so we made it work and will be spending Christmas with our families in town, where it all started.

I have to admit that it feels even more special to be back this year. I'm finally working on my own and I'm doing really well for my first venture. I moved to Chicago after my summer internship and found another company to take me on those first couple of years after graduating. Some may say Knox had a little helping hand with that. He knows a lot of people there, and it was easier to get a foot in with him by my side. And I love the home we've created for ourselves there. We have a house now, just outside the city, and we've made friends that we often meet for drinks and bowling, and all types of cheesy, couple-y activities. I'm happy with where our life is going and can't wait to see what else is in store for us.

Pushing the kitchen door back, I shout, "What's a daughter gotta do to be fed around here?"

My dad drops the wooden spoon he's using to stir something in a pot and takes his hands to his chest. "Mo stór! Oh my! You're gonna give me a heart attack! What are you doing here?"

My mom comes out of the pantry and stops in her tracks when she sees me, "Oh, Triona! Why didn't you tell us you were coming?"

I move towards them both, giving each a hug that shows them how much I've missed them, and tell them, "I wanted to surprise you guys! We don't have a lot of time off because of Knox's next game, but we still wanted to come see you."

"Oh, I'm so happy you're here, honey." My dad wraps me in another hug, his voice cracking.

"And I'm so excited to see you guys! I haven't seen you since the summer, and you already look different to me."

"What? Do I have more whites in my hair?" mom asks, lowering her head for me to look at her roots.

I laugh, "No, of course you don't. I'm just joking… I just meant that I missed you."

"Now, that I know is true!" my dad says. "Go take a seat at the bar, and I'll whip something up for you. Are you hungry?"

I hold my stomach, "Starving!"

"Are you guys expecting everyone in town tomorrow?" I ask my mom once we're both at the bar, me sitting and she wiping the counter.

"Probably, yeah. Just like every year, honey." She moves around the counter and comes to sit next to me. "So you're staying until Christmas' Day? Is Knox joining us on Christmas' Eve?"

"Yeah, we have to leave on Christmas' Day, but only in the evening, so we still have time to spend together, mom. And Knox will be with his parents, but he'll come over for a few hours tomorrow and the day after, if that's okay with you."

"Of course it is, honey, your aunts will be happy to see him."

We talk for a while and when my dad joins us, I update them on what we've been up to in the last few days. When it's past 9pm, I tell them I'm tired and that I'll have Knox pick me up. They're also going home early tonight, but my mom always likes to do a few extra things the night before the luncheon, so I know not to expect them home for another couple of hours.

"Hey you", he smiles at me. "Did you miss me?"

"Yep! Sure did." I buckle my belt and hand him a paper bag, "Dad made it for you. He said you need to keep your strength up to play the next game."

"Ohh, that man knows what I need. Smells great!"

We make our way through main street, driving towards my parents' house, where we're staying for the next couple of nights. When we get closer, instead of turning right to my street, he turns left.

"Oxie, have you forgotten where I live?"

He glares at me, a hurt look on his face, "No, I know exactly where you *live*... with me. In Chicago."

I chuckle, "You know I meant where my parents live. But seriously, you should have turned right."

"I'm taking you someplace else first," he says, kissing my knuckles.

After a couple more minutes driving away from the town, I realize where he's taking me. I see the clearing ahead, and the exact spot I had to pee in a bush once, which also gave me a rash.

"Oxie! I can't believe you!" I have tears in my eyes. He's incredibly thoughtful. That's one of the things I had to re-learn how to let him do these things for me. I had to let myself be taken care of by him again. He's always thinking about ways to surprise me on the daily basis. Bringing me chocolate, buying purple flowers, bringing me a cup of coffee when I'm working late, massaging my shoulders, and getting me random trinkets he finds. We now have a huge collection of Mystery Machines, adorning my office space.

He opens the back door and grabs a few things before telling me, "What are you waiting for? Come on!"

I giggle, so excited about what's happening. When I meet him at the bed of his truck, he has propped two pillows up against the frame and he has two blankets on his hands that he's also layering down. Then, he picks up a thermos and tells me to climb up. "Do you need any help, girlfriend of mine?"

"Nope! But I wouldn't mind some help later..." I wink at him.

We lay there, under our blankets, staring at the stars for at least an hour. We talk about nothing in particular, the rhythm of our breaths matching each other. His deep questions about the universe don't surprise me anymore, but I still cherish them more than ever. Before we leave, we make love under the stars, the same place where we learned to love each other back in high school.

The Christmas' luncheon went by without a hitch. The whole town went over for their feast and left happy and with heavy stomachs. Knox came over for a few hours on Christmas' Eve to spend time with my aunts and uncle, but he left to have dinner with his parents and family. We all agreed to throw a large party next year, with both families coming together.

It's Christmas' Day now and I woke up later than I had planned, but still in time to find my parents enjoying their cup of tea together at the kitchen island. I loved spending time with them on days like this, taking things slow before the big rush of everyone coming over again. We prepare the main dish together, singing Christmas carols and having fun. My mom still manages to sneak behind my dad's back and taste the stew before adding a few spices she believes will enhance its flavor. My dad catches her, for the millionth time, and then I'm having to intervene and remind them they love each other.

I chuckle to myself. A relationship really isn't all smooth sailing, but if everything Knox and I fight over are spices, well, I'll be happy to let him do all the cooking.

Later, when everyone is fed, I go upstairs to my bedroom and start tidying it and packing the two or three things we brought in a totebag. Looking around the walls, I see mementos that take me back in time and feel a bit teary. It's always nice to be back, but always difficult to see how far you've come. Even if these changes are all positive and great, you still miss how things used to be. Seeing an old photo of Sienna, Liv and I, I snap a picture of it with my phone and share it in our 'three musketeers' group, messaging them 'I can't believe how young we looked!'

'I looked just as hot as I do now', Liv messages back.

'Owww, we were so cute!', Sienna adds.

'Let's chat tomorrow when I'm back?', I type.

Once we've made plans for what time we'll all be free, I sit on my bed and look around to make sure I haven't forgotten anything. I'm just taking another sweep across the room when I hear a tapping sound.

Giggling to myself, recognizing it right away, I stand up and walk over to my window. Opening it, I shout at him, "What are you doing, Oxie? The front door's working!"

"I thought I'd boombox you from down here. Do you have a speaker?"

I laugh at him. "No! Get your ass up here!"

"Can't do…" he shrugs, "Gotta take my girl somewhere."

Confused, I ask him, "What? Where?"

"You'll see…" he jerks again.

"But Knox, we gotta leave soon. You wanna be back before tomorrow morning, remember?"

"Ina, bring your beautiful ass down here, please," then he adds, "Use the front door."

Making my way downstairs, I grab my jacket and tell my parents I'll be right back.

"You look beautiful," he tells me when I reach him by the car.

"What's up with you? I'm literally wearing what you saw me with yesterday", I giggle, blushing with his comment. I'm still not used to his compliments, even though he shares them with me every day.

"Well, you look gorgeous, and I hadn't told you that yet today." He grabs my waist and pulls me into him, smelling the top of my head like he loves doing. "Are you ready?"

"I don't even know what's happening. What should I be ready for?" I push him away, my hands against his chest.

A huge smile on his face, with that dimple that I die for, he says, "You'll see.. C'mon! Get in."

He jumps into the truck and turns the engine on before I can even make my way around to the passenger seat. Once I climb in, he starts driving and I can sense something weird's about to happen. He has this nervous energy that I rarely see in him. Even before important games, he doesn't feel like this. I'm looking at him, watching him drive and I wonder if I should be worried. Is there something wrong? Before I can let my thoughts overtake me, he's parking the truck.

"Wha-? Why are we here? It's freezing today", I tell him, looking over my right and wondering why we're at the Swing, our local bonfire slash lake area.

He opens and closes the door without saying a word, and I follow him, confused.

"Knox, what's happening? Why are we here?" I ask him, my voice thick with concern now.

He smiles brightly at me and says, "Come with me." He offers me his right hand and takes me closer to the lake. I see the wooden chairs that are always there and we make our way towards them. He drops onto one and gestures that I do the same.

"Are you feeling okay? Should I be worried?" I ask him. He must know how confused I feel because he loses no time to reassure me.

Putting his right hand on top of my left one, he starts, "I really wanted to come here today. I mean, look at this view." I look towards the lake, the soft undulations making the most familiar sounds. "You know it's been over 12 years since we met, right here?" He asks, not looking for an answer. "These past few years have been the best I've had in my life, but that night, when I almost kicked you into hating me forever, I knew then that my life had already changed." He pauses for 1, 2, 3, 4, 5… 6 seconds, before continuing, "I knew the second I laid my eyes on you that you would be in charge of changing my future forever."

He stands up now, then kneels in front of me and grabs my hands in his. "I could have never predicted what happened, but I knew by the way you stood by me, how you motivated me and cheered me on when the days were dark, I knew that I wanted to do life with you." He looks me in the eyes, his clear green now, "I really wanted to come here today. To make a new beginning with you."

"Triona Gallagher, I promise to always be honest with you, to continue being vulnerable and open with you. I promise I will ask you weird questions every day, and I promise I will continue taking the longest showers, as long as you're in there with me. If we're lucky enough one day, I promise to raise our kids in red and black, and take them around the world to show them how talented their mom is. I promise to love you and help you, and to slow down and care for our relationship when life gets in the way." With tears in his eyes, he puts his hand inside his front pocket, removes something and finishes, "More importantly, I promise I'll give you every single cliché life has to offer. Will you, please, do life with me? Will you marry me, Ina?"

The next few minutes are a blur. In between my tears and my racing heart, I jump to him, hugging him and knocking us both down to the ground. Our kisses are wet and salty, but our souls feel right at home.

"Yes, 3002 times yes, Oxie."

Acknowledgments

This book could not be done without the sleepless hours of some of my favorite people in the world: Bea, Mari and Loïc. Thank you, guys, for reading and re-reading my story, not holding back with feedback and for always, always reassuring me I can do this. This novel would not be in your hands without them, and I would like to take a moment to applaud them three.

*

Clap, clap!

*

I never saw this day actually being a part of my life, so in the words of a great, American philosopher, *"I want to thank me for believing in me, I want to thank me for doing all this hard work. I wanna thank me for having no days off. I wanna thank me for never quitting. I wanna thank me for always been a giver and trying to give more than I receive. I want to thank me for trying to do more right than wrong. I want to thank me for just being me at all times."* – Snoop Dogg

Author Bio

Catarina M. Szymanski is a lover of all things cozy, prefers to stay at home with a romance novel and a cup of coffee rather than making plans with the friends she misses terribly. A lifelong storyteller, she's been crafting stories about princesses slaying dragons ever since she realized she could make her younger sister laugh and daydream. Her hobbies include painting, making lists, organizing just for the fun of it, and re-watching her favorite TV shows. "Words speak louder than actions" is her reinvented favorite quote, *words of affirmation* being her love language, after all.

Meet me @catarinamswrites on Instagram and join my readers' list to be the first one to receive news, updates and more!

www.ingramcontent.com/pod-product-compliance
Lightning Source LLC
Chambersburg PA
CBHW020958160726
47994CB00006B/2281